D1577757

FOOD FAIR FRENZY

FOOD FAIR FRENZY

BOOK IV

Abby L. Vandiver

Find me on my website: www.abbyvandiver.com
Follow me on Twitter: @AbbyVandiver
Facebook: www.facebook.com/authorabbyl.vandiver

Cover Design by Shondra C. Longino

ISBN-13: 978152130715

First Printing June 2017
Printed in the United States

10 9 8 7 6 5 4 3 2 1

Dedication

To my mother. Love you always.

Chapter One
Freemont County, Georgia
Annual Possum Pickin' Food Fair

I stopped, fork mid-way to my widely-opened mouth, and let my eyes dart around the inside of the crowded tent. People had suddenly started moaning and groaning. A handful of them were bent over grabbing their stomachs. Faces a fluorescent pink, there were beads of sweat popping up on their foreheads as they coughed and spat. I couldn't be sure if the droppings of red dribble coming from their mouths were from what they ate, or blood.

What the hey . . .

And then the first one dropped.

It was a man. He wore a short-sleeved white shirt, gray pants, and a straw hat that fluttered away as he fell. He hit the ground hard, clutching his chest. He started writhing around in the dirt, grunting and panting, his body twitching, seemingly wrenched in pain. Laying next to him was a red-rimmed paper plate with a slice of pie that looked eerily familiar.

I glanced down at the plate in my hand. It had a huge slice of flaky-crusted, shiny, sugary cherry pie.

Same kind as "Sick Guy." The red stain of that last bite still smeared across his lips.

Oh crap.

I dropped the fork onto the plate, and chucked it, pie and all, into a nearby 10-gallon, garbage lined, plastic trash can as I trotted over to see about Sick Guy. I reached him just as another pie partaker hit the dust with a thud and a whimper. A woman this time – her pie sliding across the dirt floor, landing near where I knelt.

How could something that looked so good, be this bad?

I stole a quick glance in the newly sick person's direction. She'd have to wait, I determined, as I dumped the pie off of Sick Guy's plate and used it as a fan. He had been the first to fall.

"Can someone call for help?" I yelled to no one in particular. I was trying to stay calm. "Anyone that's not sick," I said, thinking I should clarify. "Please," I eked out an octave higher. "Someone, please get some help."

People were staring at me, the well ones, mouths gaped open, seemingly not knowing what to do. "It's the pie," I said, ninety-nine percent sure that it was. "We need to get a doctor in here."

Now even the sick ones, glassy-eyed, turned to stare at me, silently seeking help as another one hit the ground. Faces confused, pie plates still in hand.

I let out a long sigh and looked around. No one had died yet, thank goodness. But with all the bodies that had been piling up around me in the last few months, I was sure that Death #6 was imminent.

I was inside a huge red and white striped tent. I had followed a steady stream of fair attendees past a gigantic sign near the entrance flap that had welcomed us to "A Plethora of Pies."

It was the 105th Freemont County Annual Possum Pickin' Food Fair. My first, and from the look of things as I knelt beside Sick Guy, his crimson-colored face pouring with sweat, it would be my last.

A hot August day, clear blue skies and a small breeze off the Savannah, it had been the perfect day to be outside. Lincoln Park, where the fair was located, was filled with scores of tents to visit with a vast array of delectable dishes. I hadn't run into any possum dishes yet, but then again, I had steered away from the meat-on-a-stick peddlers just in case.

Some contestants had brought their wares from as far as six counties over, or so I'd been told, to enter the coveted contest held every year. Three days of tasting that would culminate into a winner in each of the three "S" categories – Sweet, Savory, and On-A-Stick. As I glanced toward the trash overrun with red-rimmed plates, I was pretty sure the cherry pie wouldn't make it into the finals.

There were at least a dozen of pie booths underneath the big top, all with catchy names and offerings of every kind. The sign over the counter at ground zero though, said it all. It read, "Aunt Martha's Cherry Pie to Die For."

Looks like that sign just may be literal.

And it was a brown haired, wide-eyed, Aunt Martha, I guessed, that came running. She had emerged from a curtain at the back of her pie area that I figured must be used for prep. Her face flush, hands flailing, she was donned in a frilly, salmon pink apron tied neatly over a yellow blouse, and brown polyester slacks. Her black orthopedic shoes came to a halt next to the prone body of Sick Guy where she promptly let out a loud grunt.

"Did you call for help?" I asked glancing up at her from my fanning.

She dropped to her knees and placed her hand on Sick Guy's chest, and then looked at me. "What in the tarnation is going on?" she screeched.

"Seems like your pie is making them sick," I said. *Isn't that obvious?*

"There's no way my pie did this," she cut a look at me. "You're fine and I just served it to you."

"I didn't eat it," I said. "Not after it turned out to really be 'pie to die for.'"

"You hush up now," she hissed at me. "That's ridiculous. My pie couldn't hurt anyone." Aunt Martha's face turned as red as her pie. "My pies have won awards. Lots of them. I have a curio filled with blue ribbons," she said, her voice lowered, her tone turning indignant. "I've taken top prize every time I've entered them in any contest."

"Well, I don't think you'll be winning any ribbons this go round," I said halting the makeshift fan over

Sick Guy just long enough to wipe his face with a paper napkin I found nearby. "In fact, I wouldn't be surprised if you and your pie landed in a jail cell."

She huffed, and with another grunt pushed herself up from the ground. "There is no way my pie could have done this." She brushed her hands over her apron, spun on thick soled shoes, and marched back behind her counter. "Marigold," she yelled.

"Can you get some help?" I shouted after her as I crawled over to Aunt Martha's second casualty. "I saw a medical tent out there." I pointed to the fairgrounds and took to waving the plate in front of the woman's face.

"Marigold!" she shrieked again.

Why she was shouting for "Marigold?" Was Marigold a doctor? Or at least a nurse?

Hopefully she is, I thought as I waved the paper plate more fervently. Because as I watched another cherry pie eater hit the ground, I knew I couldn't keep this fanning up much longer.

Chapter Two

"She said it was my pie," Aunt Martha said to a security guard, pointing her finger at me. "My pie is the best in the fair." She wiped her eyes, then dabbed at her nose. Her dour persona suddenly transformed into one of vulnerability, complete with tears. The performance, I was convinced, was to just raise suspicion on me.

A younger woman, blonde, with eyes that looked purple as a glint of sunlight hit her glasses, and bubble gum colored glossy lips stood next to her. She wore a vibrantly-colored, flowered mini sun dress. I chuckled. I knew if Miss Vivee saw her she'd say, "That dress is so short, I can see all the way up to Christmas."

Bubble-gum Girl rubbed Aunt Martha's back, seemingly to help settle her spurious emotional upheaval, all while Aunt Martha's baby blues shot daggers at me. I assumed Bubble-Gum Girl must be Marigold. She had come to Aunt Martha's aid, and it appeared took her word without any evidence that I was to blame for the uproar.

I guessed from her actions, or rather non-action as Martha's pie eaters still fell all around her, she had no medical training. It didn't matter to me. I had given up on fanning once the medics arrived.

I tried to brush the dirt off my white jean capris pants that I had been so careful all day not to get dirty. I wanted to look cute for Bay when he arrived.

My FBI boyfriend, Bay Colquett, was driving down from the Atlanta field office where he was stationed, and was supposed to meet me and his family at the fair. I had been so conscientious not to get anything on my pink and white checkered shirt, and had stood practically the whole day so my pants would stay clean. Now everything, including my pink Keds tennis shoes, was covered in dust, sweat, and pie guts.

I could forget about looking cute now.

I blew out a breath, and tugged at the ponytail holder on my hair, pulling it off, I tried to redo my hair. It was all sweated out and had started to frizz up. There was really no hope for it.

I walked by the cherry pie killer and her precious Marigold on my way to the exit and tried not to let them draw me into their drama. I kept my focus straight ahead and walked at a fast pace.

"Excuse me," the officer pointed his finger at me. "May I have a word with you?"

Geez, I thought. *Is he really going to question "me" about the killer pie?*

I let out a sigh and headed over toward the guard. This was ridiculous. Here I was, once again, talking to the law about my activities. Luckily, this time they were legal. What am I doing? I'm an archaeologist, graduated at the top of my class, and I'm lollygagging around at the "Freemont County" Possum Festival located in all places – Augusta County, when I ought to be on a dig discovering something important about our history.

I should have ditched out the tent when I ditched the pie, and never have stopped to help Sick Guy.

I saddled up next to the security guy and glanced at Aunt Martha and Marigold's smug faces. They were slowly nodding their heads as if saying, "Yes. She's the one."

"How can I help?" I said to the guard, forcing myself to keep my eyes stayed on him. I dug my hands down in my pants pockets.

"What do you know about these people getting sick?" he asked.

Oh. My. Gosh. Really?

"I don't know it for sure," I said with the most innocent face I could muster. "But from the circumstances surrounding them getting sick, I'd say it was Aunt Martha's pie that was making them keel over."

The guard had to put his arm up to block Aunt Martha from lunging at me.

"Logan."

I heard my name, and turned around to see Mac, leaning on his cane, limping my way. He hooked the cane over his arm, lifted his hat and ran his handkerchief over his head, his usual shock of white hair lying flat on its own. Probably from the sweat I noticed glistening on his forehead.

"Thought I'd come and see if I could be of some assistance," Mac said as he approached, placing his straw Panama back on and tugging at its brim. "Seems as if there are more people getting sick then there are people to help." Mac looked around the tent as the medics busied themselves with the fallen pie prey.

"Dr. Whitson," the security guard seemed to recognize Mac. "Glad you're here. Not one of those first aid people are actually doctors."

"Hello, my good man." It was evident that Mac didn't know him. "Glad to be of assistance."

"Do you know her?" the misinformed guard said pointing to me.

"Of course I do. She's my granddaughter," Mac said with a proud face. He probably felt that way about me, but everyone else did a quick jerk of their heads. I was sure they wanted to know how Mac could be my grandfather when I was black, and his tale-tell pale skin under his hat, showed he definitely was not.

"Your granddaughter?" Aunt Martha said, skepticism in her voice. "I don't know about that, but I do know that she is the devil." She leaned in toward me as she spoke. I leaned away.

It's true. No good deed goes unpunished.

I looked into her eyes and could see how much she was upset with me. I just wanted to scream at her, "Why are you mad at me? It's not my pie that's killing everyone."

"Calm down, Martha." The security guard made his arm blockade stronger. "Marigold, you want to help me with your grandmother?"

Mac looked at me and then at the guard. "I came to see if I could help," he said. "But I think my best effort would be put toward rescuing my granddaughter. C'mon Logan. Let's find Grandma and make sure she's okay.

I chuckled. *I guess "grandma" is Miss Vivee.*

We walked out of the tent and found people clutching their chests, holding their heads, and throwing up. Everywhere. There was a steady stream of bluish-colored people heading toward the Porta potties. Many more, it seemed, than were at the Plethora of Pies. And, I might add, a whole different color. A quick scan of the area, and it was obvious that Aunt Martha's pie wasn't the only food people were dying for. I glanced over and saw a lethargic group near one of the Meat-on-A Stick tents. Turning, I headed in the opposite direction.

"What is going on around here?" I said to Mac.

"I don't know." He looked around the fair grounds. "But be sure to stay away from fair food."

I chuckled and said, "No problem there."

"Vivee packed me some goose liver and onion sandwiches," he smiled and patted my arm. "So don't worry, you won't starve. I'll be happy to share one with you when we get back."

Lord give me strength, I thought and tried to return the smile. But I was sure, if I ate one of those things, I'd be the next one to turn blue and pass out.

Chapter Three

"Excuse me, Ma'am," we heard a man say as we walked up to our picnic area. "I have something for Vivienne Pennywell."

Mac and I had pushed past the tide of fairgoers that had become frenzied after pie eaters and others had gotten sick. I was happy to be back. I wanted to make sure no one in our group had eaten any of the Freemont County Possum Pickin's deadly fare.

The fair grounds were huge, and we had picked an area on the outskirts and pitched a canopy tent with flap drop walls. We had several small tables, a cooler for water and Miss Vivee's food – her usual egg salad and now I'd discovered, goose liver and onion sandwiches. There were several folding quad chairs and a prep table for Renmar's entries into the cooking contests.

The man wanting to give Miss Vivee something was probably somewhere in his early twenties. Trying to get her attention, he couldn't seem to get past her daughters, Renmar Colquett and Brie Pennywell, who stood rooted firm as oak trees in front of her. Arms crossed, they created a protective, unmovable force field.

"May I help you?" Renmar asked, eyebrows raised, lips pursed.

Renmar was the epitome of a southern belle. Her hair was always in place, her clothes smart and stylish. Today, she had on a white tennis skirt, and a navy blue Polo shirt. I'd never seen her without make-up, or a ready smile, and a kind word while around others.

For the most part, she ran the Maypop Bed & Breakfast, the family owned business where we all lived, but she also was a cook extraordinaire. And she was Bay's doting mother and, particularly protective over her mother, Miss Vivee, who could be a real firecracker.

Juxtaposed against Renmar, the Fair Ground Guy looked grubby. He wore a scruffy stubble on his face, and had a mountain of curly black hair. He was long-legged and slim. His clothes – khaki pants, and a ceil blue, button-down shirt with a Freemont County logo on it – looked rumpled. But there was an "Official" badge on a lanyard around his neck, seemingly making his intrusion authorized and someone not to be ignored – at least by fairground standards.

Nonetheless, he couldn't get through. He seemed anxious, and aiming to circumvent the Wall of Guardian Daughters solicited an appeal to Miss Vivee. "I have something for you, Mrs. Pennywell," he said and flapped a piece of paper.

"Who are you?" Renmar questioned.

"I'm Gavin Tanner," he said looking flustered. "A fair official." He wiggled his badge, and sighed. "I have something for her." He emphasized the last part of his sentence and pointed at Miss Vivee.

"What is going on?" I said and stood next to Official Guy Gavin Tanner.

Miss Vivee leaned to one side of her chair when she heard my voice, peering around Brie's large curves and looked at me.

There she was. *Grandma.*

I noticed the little grin on her face. Whatever was going on, she was enjoying it. She had on two pairs of glasses – her sunglasses sitting atop her prescription ones. She wore a straw hat, with a floppy, frayed brim, and a blue ribbon tied around it. Even in the 90 degree heat, she had on her signature round collar, blue coat. Her long white braid was pulled over her shoulder and Cat, her wheaten Scottish terrier, sat at her feet.

Looking much more "elderly," than her usual self-professed Voodoo herbalist, take-no-mess-from-anyone, nonagenarian self, I knew Miss Vivee was up to something.

Official Guy looked at me with eyes that pleaded for assistance.

"What do you need?" I asked.

"We need Mrs. Pennywell to see if she can understand what this means." He rattled a piece of paper covered in plastic in front of me.

"What is it?" I said and tried to pry it from his fingers. He wouldn't let it go.

"It's for Mrs. Pennywell. No one else."

"We'll take it," Brie said, and stuck out her hand.

"What is it about?" I directed my question to the fair official, but Brie answered.

"Who knows," she said. "Who cares? Momma can't be burdened with all these things."

What things? I thought. *It's just a piece of paper.*

"I know what it's about," Renmar said. "It's about what mother did last year. They probably want her gone, and then there goes my entries into the contest."

"What did she do?" I asked.

Just like Miss Vivee to get thrown out of someplace steeped in tradition.

"It's about the people getting sick. At the food tents," Gavin interjected into our conjecturing. "We think this might have something to do with that."

"Has anyone died?" Miss Vivee's first words. I looked over at her. She had leaned out further this time. I hoped she didn't tumble out of that folding chair.

"No!" he said taken aback and looked at her questioningly "No one's died." He shook his head and swallowed." But it might be a clue as to what happened to make all those people sick."

"Oh." Renmar seemed relieved. She relaxed her stance, stood aside, and looked at Miss Vivee. "Mother, are you going to help them? Seems like a pretty important matter." Renmar gave a fake smile and ran her fingers through her bobbed brown hair.

15

"You'd give in, throw your mother to the wolves, wouldn't you?" Miss Vivee asked Renmar. "If it meant your 7-Up cake didn't miss the judging."

"That's not true, Mother. And I'm not throwing you to the wolves. He works for Lincoln Park."

"Nope," Miss Vivee said. I couldn't see her eyes behind her double pair of glasses, but I'm sure there was a twinkle in those blue eyes of hers. "I'm not going to help."

"Mother," Renmar said. "This is important." She looked at the Fair Official Guy. "Isn't it?"

"Yes ma'am," he said and gave a nod.

"Don't care," Miss Vivee said. "They can't make me, and I won't do it." She crossed her arms.

"How can you not help, Miss Vivee?" I asked. "I was over there by the pie tent and it was bad. People getting sick. Falling out. It was really bad."

"But no one died," she said, and looked over at Fair Official Gavin for confirmation.

He shook his head "no" again.

"This is a sick person doing this," Miss Vivee said rebelliously. "And I won't give in to the whims of a deranged individual."

"You don't know they're deranged, Miss Vivee," I said.

"They made people sick and then sent a note about it? That sounds sick to me," she said. She bent down and picked up Cat and put her on her lap. She patted her dog. "I won't be a part of it."

"Mother," Renmar said. She used a calm, composed voice. "They're counting on you. You should be very proud of that. Plus, it's your civic duty to help."

"Look who's talking," Miss Vivee said to Renmar. "Doing your civic duty is not hiding extinct fish for twenty years."

"I had no idea they were extinct," Renmar said, hurt showing in her eyes, obviously her mother's words bringing back an unpleasant memory.

"They weren't extinct," Mac said. "Not if they'd been swimming in that creek all that time."

"You," Miss Vivee pointed a bony, shaky finger at Mac. "Stay out of it."

"Momma," Brie said. "Be nice."

"You're good at solving things like this, as much as I hate to admit it," Renmar said. "You should help."

Miss Vivee didn't budge.

"Logan," Renmar looked at me. "You talk to her, she listens to you."

Everyone looked at me expectedly, including Miss Vivee.

They should know that Miss Vivee didn't listen to me, or for that matter, to anyone. I don't think that she even followed any kind of plan in her head. She acted off the cuff, and usually in direct contradiction to how everyone else thought things should be.

"How about if I just take you home, Miss Vivee," I said. "I think the sun and the day has been too much for you." Thought I'd try a little reverse psychology.

"All these people worrying you." I patted my leg for Cat to come over to me. He jumped off her lap and circled my legs.

At least someone was cooperating.

Then I reached out to give Miss Vivee a hand and help her out of the chair.

She swatted my hand away. "Oh my Lord. I hope I don't throw up," Miss Vivee said. "All this hullabaloo over some pie." She smacked her lips. "Two minutes ago," Miss Vivee looked at Renmar. "When you thought it was about that god-blasted cake of yours, you wouldn't let the man near me."

I had to hide my chuckle.

"Give me the note." Miss Vivee waggled her fingers, reaching for it. But before he could, another "Official" came up and whispered in Gavin Tanner's ear.

The man's eyes darted from Renmar to Brie, and then over to me. He opened his mouth to speak, but let it snap shut.

"What is it?" Renmar asked.

Gavin looked at Official Guy #2, who took the note from his hand. "I apologize for the inconvenience, ma'am but I don't think we'll need you anymore." New Official Guy-in-Charge nodded his head, and tugged on Gavin's arm.

"If you'll excuse us . . ." He bowed out and walked away, Official Gavin following behind.

We watched, but before they got out of our view, we saw Yasamee's sheriff, Lloyd Haynes stop them.

They whispered among themselves for a few moments, and then they all turned back and looked at us.

Lloyd came over. He took off his four-dented brown hat, and brushed back the tuft of chestnut hair that had fallen in his face. His usually crisp tan-colored uniform shirt was damp from his sweat, and I could see him tighten the muscle in his square jaw line as he readied to speak.

"What's going on?" Brie asked before he could even get any words out.

"We're gonna need Miss Vivee," he said, his brown eyes showing his seriousness.

"Is this about what happened last year?" Renmar was back on that seemingly oblivious to his tone and demeanor. "Because I did pay the restitution that they required-"

Lloyd held up his hand stopping her mid-sentence. "Miss Vivee, will you come with me? I need you in the Judges Tent." He walked over to her and put out his hand, you could see his solid triceps muscle flex through his short sleeve shirt as he grabbed her and pulled her up. Then he looked at Mac. "We're going to need you, too."

"Is someone dead?" Miss Vivee asked again. She seemed hopeful.

"Yes," Sheriff Haynes said. "And it might just be another murder."

Chapter Four

Of course it would be murder. What else would it be?

Since I'd met Miss Vivee that's all I'd seen. As an archaeologist, I usually dug up dead bodies, but with Miss Vivee around they were just dropping at my feet.

Miss Vivee wasn't morbid or a psychopath, I knew that for sure, but it sure would seem odd, I know, to any onlooker how she acted. She hadn't wanted to help when it was people getting sick, but now that she'd heard "murder," she was raring to go.

Whatever Miss Vivee had done last year at the annual food fair, and I could only imagine, all had seemed to be forgiven. They came for her help at the first sign of trouble. And even though she had no official capacity – as anything – Sheriff Haynes had come for her and Mac first thing.

Macomber "Mac" Whitson was easy to understand getting high clearance, he was a doctor. The only MD, apparently, at the food fair. But Miss Vivee's only expertise, besides always turning up at the scene of a murder, was that she was a Voodoo herbalist. Sick in love or health, she proclaimed she had the powers to put one out of their misery. Literally, I'm told. But I must admit, Miss Vivee did have a knack for just looking at a dead body and knowing what had caused its death. That kind of power sure would come in handy in my profession.

"Hey. What'd I miss?" Hazel Cobb came through the flap on the canopy tent, her dark brown skin glistening from being out in the sun. "I just saw Sheriff Lloyd Haynes walking with Miss Vivee and Mac. Is something wrong?"

"Mother doesn't need to get involved with any of this," Renmar said. She walked over to the ice filled cooler and took out a big glass, gallon-jar of lemonade. "You know how she gets all involved with those murders, thinking she can solve them."

She does solve them, I thought to myself. She and Mac could have their own amateur sleuth, crime solving, hour of elderly brain power, television show. It would soar in the ratings department. Betty White meets Angela Lansbury, with Andy Griffith as the sidekick.

"Murder?" Hazel Cobb asked and pulled two red Solo cups out the plastic, holding it for Renmar to pour. "Who in the world has been murdered now?"

"I just won't have it," Renmar continued, ignoring Hazel's questions. "And Brie, how could you let Lloyd take Mother away like that?" She sat down in one of the chairs and Hazel Cobb sat down beside her.

"Me!" Brie said. "What makes you think I could have any control over that? Or him? That's his job."

"Isn't he your boyfriend?" Renmar asked.

That one took me by surprise. I looked over at Brie who was turning beet red.

"I . . ." she said and then seemed stuck for words.

"Oh everyone knows." Renmar waved her hand. "Don't try to hide it."

I didn't know.

"Renmar, don't be so crass," Hazel said. "She called herself keeping it a secret."

"Well, she should have done a better job of it."

"I'm sitting right here, you know," Brie said.

I looked at Brie. She did look different lately. Her usual motherly-like frocks and French rolled hair were gone. She had her light brown tresses brushed in soft curls that framed her face, her freckles were nearly hidden under a light dusting of face powder, and a frosted coral gloss covered her lips. She wore a light blue skort, showing off surprisingly shapely legs. Her matching tank top showed her tanned arms and ample cleavage. For the first time since I'd met her, I thought she looked pretty. I smiled.

Brie's got a boyfriend. How cute.

"All I know is we came here to have fun," Brie said finding her words.

Like me, Brie was the baby in the family and for the most part acquiesced to Renmar on everything. Dating, though, seemed to have helped her find her footing against her big sister.

"But if Lloyd -" Brie cleared her throat. "Sheriff Haynes needs her. What's the harm?"

Plus, I thought. *Who could stop Miss Vivee from doing what she wanted to do?*

"And what was on that note?" Renmar said. "Why did they need Mother to look at it?"

Hazel swallowed a gulp of lemonade. "What note?" she asked. She still hadn't been briefed on the goings on.

I wondered what could be on it, too. What could be written on a note that would give answers for what I'd seen in the Plethora of Pie tent?

"I just won't have it," Renmar mumbled her feelings again.

Renmar thought Miss Vivee needed protecting. She was, in Renmar's mind, old and feeble. She was no longer able to make good decision on her own, and she treated her as such. Bay had told me that Miss Vivee needed protecting, too, but for a different reason. He wanted to shield others from keeping her from being independent. Exactly what he thought his mother was trying to do. All their coddling of her though, no matter the reason, didn't help. Miss Vivee could not be controlled.

My opinion, in the small amount of time I'd spent with Miss Vivee, was that she didn't need any help from anyone, for anything. She had a mind of her own and it wasn't one to be toyed with. I knew that both Renmar and Bay meant well, but their actions just helped fuel Miss Vivee's fire. I think she did more things – took more risks – just to upset them.

"Logan!" Renmar jolted me from my thoughts. "You go and see about Mother."

"Me?"

"Yes. You. And fix yourself." I stood up and she waved her hand up and down at me. "You look a mess. Is that the way you want Bay to see you?"

I looked down and brushed off the front of my clothes. "I was trying to help the sick people in the pie tent," I said in a whiny voice that even surprised me.

"That's really no excuse, Sweetie. I'm sure you could've helped without getting so dirty."

"Oh leave her alone, Renmar," Brie said and smiled at me. "That's what she does. Gets dirty. She's an archaeologist."

"Not today she isn't. She's representing the Colquett and Pennywell family." She looked at me. "So skedaddle! Go check on Mother and make sure she isn't dragging our good name through the mud."

Renmar, just like me, knew there was no stopping Miss Vivee, although she never gave up trying, or relegating me the chore of putting a halt to her antics. I'd thought it a good idea anyway to at least go make sure she didn't cause too much trouble.

I walked toward the judges' tent where they had taken Miss Vivee and Mac. As I had passed by the Plethora of Pie tent, I saw that it was empty. The artificial lights were off, no sweet smell wafted from inside the flap, and it seemed chillingly quiet after the earlier kerfuffle. I didn't see that Aunt Martha or her precious, unhelpful Marigold anywhere, either.

Once I got to the tent where the Sheriff had taken Miss Vivee, I saw that judging was going on right outside of it. There was a stage with a table and three people – two woman and a man sitting at it, and one empty chair. A woman was at the microphone, her southern drawl was filled with gentility. She wore her honey brown frosted hair in a Justin Bieber cut, and donned large solitaire diamond earrings, and a high-count carat-filled tennis bracelet, all a bit much for her casual blue jeans, tank top, and wedge sandals outfit. She was announcing winners and awarding blue, red, and white ribbons. The audience was seated in white wooden folding chairs, all of them cheering and laughing, apparently having a good ole time.

Well. Doesn't anyone know about the dead body?

I pulled back the flap on the tent and stepped inside. The first person I saw was my Bay. I took my hand and tried to smooth down my hair. I tugged on my shirt and licked my lips. I wished I could look in a mirror.

Darn that Renmar.

He smiled at me and nodded. He was dressed casually in blue jeans, and a sage green button down shirt. He looked so handsome. No way I could go anywhere with him looking like I did.

Bay stroked the chin of his smooth, honey-colored skin, and scrutinized the crime scene with those hazel eyes of his that always seemed to sparkle.

Okay, maybe they just seemed to sparkle to me.

I eased up next to Mac and nudged him. "Is it really another murder?" I asked, hoping that it wasn't.

"Seems like it," Mac said.

"Oh, man," I said and shook my head.

"When did Bay get here?" I asked. "I didn't see him."

"He entered the fairgrounds on his way to our picnic area, but got sidetracked by Sheriff Haynes."

"Oh," I said and nodded.

"He hadn't forgotten about you," he said and rubbed my arm.

I smiled. "I didn't think he had." I pointed to what I assumed was the body. It was on the dirt floor underneath a white paper table cloth. "So who's the stiff?"

"He was one of the judges for the sweet contest. Apparently whatever he tasted didn't sit too well with him."

"Yeah," I said. "A lot of that's been going around."

Mac chuckled. "Best to stick with my goose liver and onion sandwiches."

"So who was he?" I asked.

"From what I've heard, he was a bigwig around here."

"Oh yeah?"

"That's what they're saying. Very rich. Very important."

I wonder what he was doing at this little Podunk county fair.

"What was his name?" I asked.

"Jack Wagner."

I never heard of him, but with me not being from around there, that wasn't strange. I'd bet Miss Vivee knew who he was, though.

Miss Vivee claimed to be a hundred years old. Her daughters, who weren't sure how old she was, thought she was probably in her nineties.

How could you not know how old your mother is?

Back home in Ohio, everyone in my family knew each other's ages. We'd write it on birthday cakes, and proudly announce it every chance we'd get. But Renmar said around here it wasn't polite to talk about a woman's age. Well, at least for everyone else because Miss Vivee talked about it all the time. Not that what she professed to be was the actual truth, but no matter how old she was, she definitely had lived long enough to know just about everyone around.

I looked over at Miss Vivee. They had gotten her a seat and were stepping around her gingerly. She was part of the investigation. Right smack dab in the middle of it. She was holding a piece of paper in her hand and was taking in everything they said and did.

"How'd he die?" I said.

Mac shrugged his shoulders. "His wife said he had a heart attack. He was back here at the tasting table," he pointed to a long table set alongside the back wall of the tent. "At least that's the version his wife gave."

"So, then it's *not* murder," I said. "He died from natural causes."

"I don't know," he said hesitantly. "I took a look at him. Seemed pretty fit to me, especially for a seventy-one year old man." He blew out a breath. "And then there's that note."

"What's on the note?"

"A poem."

"A poem?" I scrunched up my face.

"Yeah. Vivee's got a copy of it." He pointed his head toward her. "That means we'll get a look at it later. But from what I gathered about the note it makes the Sheriff think he was killed with a botanical poison. That's why he asked Vivee to take a look."

"So he was murdered?"

"Vivee and the Sheriff think so."

"What does Bay think?"

"You know Bay, he holds his judgment until he has all the facts. But he wouldn't go against Vivee, leastways not in public."

That was my Bay, always the defender of his grandmother.

"You would have thought his wife was the county coroner the way she made the pronouncement of the cause of death." Mac shook his head. "When the Sheriff asked if he had a history of heart problems, she said no."

"So why would she say he died of a heart attack," I asked.

"Beats me," Mac said. "That's the question of the day."

"And then you checked him, and it didn't seem like he suffered a heart attack?"

"Right."

"Where is Mrs. Wagner now?" I heard Bay voice my next question.

Ain't that cute how we think alike? I thought and smiled.

"She's the Mistress of Ceremony," Sheriff Haynes answered Bay's question. He jerked a thumb toward the outside of the tent. He seemed perturbed with her. "Once we got here, she mumbled something about the show must go on and took off."

The Mistress of Ceremony? I thought. Not the woman at the mike I saw when I walked in. No way had that woman's husband just died.

I backpedaled out of the tent to take another look at the newly widowed Mrs. Jack Wagner. Sure enough she was doing her duty as the MC, carrying on like nothing had happened.

"And the blue ribbon," she was saying, smiling as she spoke into the microphone, "for the 105th Freemont County Possum Pickin' Competition for the best sweet fare in all of South Georgia . . ."

I can't believe how composed she is . . . I thought shaking my head.

"And I'm sure this will come as no surprise to anyone . . ." Calm and collected, Mistress of Ceremony Wagner, raised her hand to quiet the crowd that had erupted in applause. "The winner, for her always delicious, ever scrumptious, cherry delight pie to die for, is Martha Simmons!" MC Wagner leaned in closer to the mike. "We all lovingly know her as Aunt Martha." Mrs. Wagner started clapping and the audience followed suit.

I turned to look at Aunt Martha. Her mouth opened in amazement, she slowly rose from her seat. Standing, she clutched her chest, adulation and surprise smeared across her face.

Oh my goodness!

Chapter Five

I had had enough of the fair and dead people, and was ready to go home. It may not have been a nice thing to say, but it made me happy when the coroner arrived to pick up the body. I knew Miss Vivee wouldn't have left until the very last second of the initial investigation was over, and I wasn't going to leave without her.

I had ridden to the fair with Hazel Cobb, Renmar's best friend, and Bay's cousin on his father's side. Bay and I had planned to go to dinner in Augusta after spending time at the County Fair, so I hadn't needed my Jeep. Unfortunately, now date night had now turned into work night for Bay.

I walked back over to our picnic area and found Renmar, Brie, and Hazel packing up our things. Renmar still had to wait for the judging of her bouillabaisse, and Brie had agreed to wait with her. Luckily for me Hazel said she was ready to go.

Renmar's entry in the savory category, her bouillabaisse, had won her the blue ribbon for the past seventeen years. No one spoke about it, but everyone this year was worried. For the past years' entries, Renmar had used a fish that she and now dead Oliver Gibbons, her friend and town playboy, found on Stallings Island. Little did they know, as she had just explained to her mother, it was the only fish of its kind was thought to be extinct. Once it was rediscovered, there was no way she could get her hands on it, especially to put into a fish stew. She had to kiss that secret recipe goodbye.

"Where's Mother," Renmar asked. "I thought you went to see about her?"

"She'll be here in a minute," I said and threw my thumb over my shoulder, pointing behind me. "She's walking with Bay. They stopped to get spaghetti-on-a-stick."

"Didn't they close the food stations down?" Hazel asked.

"Only the ones where people got sick," I said. "The spaghetti sticks were deemed fit to eat."

"Bay's here?" Renmar asked.

"Oh, yeah," I said. I had forgotten that she hadn't seen him. "The Sheriff snagged him on his way in."

"Why didn't you go with them?" Brie asked.

"I'm not eating anything from here," I said. "Even if they did give it the okay. And I thought you guys might need some help packing up."

"No, we're good," Brie offered. "Just waiting for the savory judging to start."

"Spaghetti on a stick?" Renmar said and scrunched up her nose. "How in the world did they do that?"

"I dunno," I said and hunched my shoulders.

Miss Vivee came into the tent first, Bay right behind her, both were empty handed.

"What happened?" Brie asked. "Thought you were getting food."

"Darn thing fell on the ground as soon as Bay bought it for me," Miss Vivee said. "Just as I leaned it to bite it – *Plop!* Off it went."

Renmar and Brie laughed. Cat raised her head, ears up, tongue out, probably in reaction to the missed opportunity for food.

"Nothing funny about that," Miss Vivee said. "That thing cost six dollars." She looked at Bay. "Hope you don't think I'm going to pay you back. I barely got my face close enough to smell it."

"No, Grandmother." He chuckled. "I don't expect you to pay me back." He helped her sit in her quad chair.

"There's my baby!" Renmar said, grinning at the sight of Bay. She went over and hugged him, stretching to get her arms around his six-foot frame.

"Baby? Could a baby do this?" He leaned down and hugged back, lifting her off her feet. She giggled and smacked his arm. Putting her back down on her feet, he walked over and gave Brie a kiss, too.

"Now, tell me what all the hullabaloo going on out there is?" Renmar said pointing over to the fairgrounds. "Did somebody really die?"

"It was Jackson Wagner," he said.

"Not *the* Jack Wagner," Renmar said and then lowered her voice. "Oh my. He was supposed to judge my bouillabaisse."

"You knew him, Renmar?" I asked.

"I knew *of* him. He's old Georgia money."

"Well now he's a possible *new* homicide victim," Bay said. "Outside city limits, so my jurisdiction."

"Oh, good Lord, no!" Renmar said, in her best southern drawl. "You and Logan were supposed to go out."

"Duty calls," he said.

"How long will you have to stay?" Hazel asked. I guess someone had filled her in.

"I don't know," Bay said. "I have to interview witnesses. Forensic team already came through. So probably not too long."

"I don't know how they thought they could put spaghetti noodles on a stick anyway," Miss Vivee was still complaining.

"Don't worry, Momma," Brie said. "We've got some more of your egg salad sandwiches. I just saw a couple in the cooler . . ." She lifted the top off and searched for Miss Vivee's Siran wrapped favorite.

"Logan," Bay said. "Come walk with me." He reached out his hand.

I grabbed it and followed him out of the tent. We walked a few dozen feet away before he spoke.

"So . . ." he started, taking in a deep breath.

"You don't even have to say it," I said and smiled up at him. I rubbed my hand over the waves in his black hair. "And it's okay."

"Are you still going to be this understanding when we're married?"

"Married?" I shook my head. "I don't know how you got a job as an FBI agent. You just have no clue. I'm not marrying you."

"No?"

"No."

"Why?" he asked, bringing my hand to his mouth and kissing it gently.

"For one," I said. "You haven't asked me."

"Will you marry me?" he asked before I could finish my list.

"And, because," I said talking over him. "I just can't picture sharing my life with a man that can't eat spaghetti from a stick. That quality is at the top of my "Who-I'd-Marry-List."

"Well, technically, it was my grandmother who couldn't do it."

"Excuses, excuses," I said.

"So you don't want this two carat, emerald cut, flawless diamond I have?" He patted his pants pocket.

"You do not have -" I said, feeling my heart start to race. I smiled so wide, my face hurt. "Do you?" I reached to feel his pocket.

He caught my hand and stepped back. "You want it, don't you?"

"What?" I didn't know what to say. *Did he really just propose?* "Do I want what?" My voice cracked.

"The ring. Marriage. Me. You want it all, don't you?"

"Do you have a two carat ring in your pocket?"

"No."

I snatched my hand out of his and punched him. He threw his head back and laughed.

"Not funny," I said.

"It's only one and a half carat," he said taking my hand again. "That's all I could afford."

"Oooo. I hate you," I said. I jerked away and took off walking – briskly – back to the picnic area.

"Wait, Logan!" he said coming after me, still laughing.

"Yoohoo!" I heard Miss Vivee yell. She had emerged from behind the wall of the canopy. "Yoohoo! Bay!"

Bay caught up to me. "You're not really mad are you?" he said, still not able to suppress whatever had struck his funny bone.

"No," I said.

"'Cause remember," he held up a finger, "you started it."

"Bay!" Miss Vivee's shrill voice floated over to us.

"Go and see what your grandmother wants," I said. "And I'll deal with you later."

"Don't dish out anything you can't take, Missy," he warned, touching his finger to the tip of my nose.

"You'd be surprised how much I can take!" I said to him as he turned and trotted over to see what Miss Vivee needed. Half way over he turned around, running backwards, he blew me kisses.

Who could be mad at him? Just looking at that man does something to me. I smiled.

Before I could get back, Bay and Miss Vivee had disappeared into the tent, and now were coming back out. Bay was carrying a yellow vinyl cooler, and Miss Vivee's quad chair on one arm, and had her on his other arm. Cat followed behind, her tail wagging.

"C'mon," Miss Vivee said to me as we met. "We're leaving."

I looked at Bay. "I gotta get back to work," he said. "Murder is priority one." Miss Vivee held out her hand so I could hold it. "You two are going to ride back home with Cousin Hazel."

"Don't forget about Mac," Miss Vivee said.

"I won't." Bay reassured her. "I'll go and get him once I get you two in the car."

"I don't know where he got off to," I said. "I thought he was right behind me when I left the judges' tent."

"Probably found some young hot thing that's got his nose." Miss Vivee nodded her head as if it were some common occurrence.

"Grandmother!" Bay said.

"What? It's probably true."

37

"I think he only has eyes for you," Bay said.

"I think so, too," I said. I looked at Miss Vivee. "No. I *know* so."

"Well, it wouldn't matter one bit to me if he had," Miss Vivee said but then looked over her shoulder, conducting a quick scan of the fairgrounds.

"You know what?" I said and let go of Miss Vivee's hand. "You put your grandmother in the car, and I'll go find Mac." Bay nodded. "Be right back."

I found Mac – talking to a pretty, young woman. I almost scolded him until he introduced her as one of his old patients. He had delivered her and her six siblings he relayed. He excused himself, and we got to the car just as Bay was putting the last of Hazel Cobb's things in the trunk. Mac and I climbed in the back seat, Miss Vivee was in the front, and we waited while Hazel hugged Bay for what seemed like an eternity, as if she wouldn't ever see him again.

I sat in the back and looked out the window at them. I thought about Bay, and wondered if he really did have a ring. And was he really asking me to marry him. To spend the rest of my life with him.

Would that be such a bad thing?

But then I thought about Camren Wagner. She didn't seem to give two hoots, as Miss Vivee would say, about her husband's death. Murder or not, she was more concerned with passing out colored ribbons. Can a person be married so long that the death of their spouse doesn't bother them? Or was that just her way of covering up her pain?

Miss Vivee and Mac had loved each other a long time, but I didn't know what to make of their relationship. Mac asked her to marry him every chance he got. Miss Vivee always turned him down.

Is that what I had to look forward to in a long-term relationship? Kookiness? Then I thought about my parents. They had been married forever. My mother, a pretty famous archaeologist gave my father so much grief with her antics. But he stuck by her and they were happy. Yep, dealing with kookiness seemed to be a fixture in long-term relationship.

But is that what I want for my life?

I had never thought about settling down and getting hitched, heck, before coming to Yasamee, I never thought about having a boyfriend. I worried about getting good grades, my doctorate in Anthropology and History, and making a name in my field. My goal, and I had convinced myself it wasn't an arrogant thing to want, was to surpass my mother in name recognition in the field of archaeology. But, my father, Andrew Mase Dickerson, "Mase" for short who worried about me being "normal," finding a man, getting married and having children, kept the hope of those things for me alive.

Bay was more than any girl could hope to have, and I knew my father would approve. He was kind, considerate, funny, and he loved me unconditionally. Just like my father loved my mother. Something I knew was hard for anyone to do.

I was the youngest of my three siblings, and I acted the part most of the time - spoiled, whiny, and disagreeable. Even though most times I didn't want my mother getting into the details of my personal life, and we didn't see eye-to-eye on anything, it was her I called whenever the least little thing went wrong. I depended on her more than I cared to admit.

"Don't think I don't know what you did back there," Miss Vivee said, interrupting my thoughts. Hazel had finally gotten into the car and we'd left the fairgrounds.

"What are you talking about?" I asked.

"Telling me I was tired and needed rest in front of all those people. I'm not feeble."

"No one would ever think that about you," Hazel Cobb answered for me.

"It's not that I care. Leastways, not what they think of me," Miss Vivee said. "People will think what they want."

"Why didn't you want to look at the note?" Hazel Cobb glanced over at Miss Vivee. "Wasn't it sent to you."

"I'm not sure if it was meant for me intentionally. But that's exactly why I wouldn't look at it," Miss Vivee said. "Whoever did this is trying to control the situation. What? Do they think they're the Son of Sam – David Berkowitz? Taunting people, sending out clues?" She shook her head. "I wasn't going to let a cowardly murderer goad me into doing their bidding."

"How do you mean?" Hazel asked.

"They want to hurt people. Make a game out of it. And they want us – me – to play along." She shook her head. "I don't want no part of that."

I raised an eyebrow. "So you were just going to let people keep getting sick?"

"It's not like I had anything to do with it," she said matter-of-factly. "And it's not like I could have stopped it. The deed had been done already. And don't think just by me reading the note, the person was going to get caught."

"But you've read it now?" I asked.

"Yeah." I could hear her opening up the clasp on her purse. "Take a look at it," she said and tried to hand it back to me. She couldn't quite put her hand back far enough, so I scooted up on my seat and reached up front.

"This is a copy?" I said. It was in a clear plastic covering, which I didn't understand. It wouldn't have had a suspect's fingerprints on it.

"Yes. It's a copy," Miss Vivee said. "I told them to put plastic on it. Keep it clean while I handled it. They wanted me to study it, and see if I could figure out which one of those flowers written on that note could have killed Jack Wagner."

"Let's not get ahead of ourselves, Vivee," Mac said. "That woman is still insisting that her husband had a heart attack. So no one is sure if one of those flowers did him in or not."

"The Sheriff's words not mine," Miss Vivee said.

I looked down at the note. My lips moving as I read it silently.

Fair flowers of the field – mystery and wonder they provide,
But hidden within, the truth they belie.
Listen closely, and one can hear,
The trickery and deception that draws one near.
They mock you with their beauty, so innocent, so sweet,
But their power – no one can defeat.
So harken, and I will tell you true,
For this will be your only clue:
Nightshade and Iris' purple majesty, truly a sight to behold,
Moleplant, and Yellow Jessamine, one milky, the other gold.
Diminutive petals hold Goldenseal's power,
And striking is the Angel's Trumpet flower.
Delphinium and Aconitum, tall their blossoms proudly stand.
But the Lily of the Valley, that one's the most grande.
Its bells, so lovely, sure to please,
It is the fairest one you'll ever see.
The flowers of the field will take away your breath.
Surely in them beauty abounds, but then, so does death.

"What does it mean, Miss Vivee?" I passed it to Mac so he could take a look at it.

"What?"

"The poem."

"I don't know," she said.

"Is this what made everyone sick?" I leaned forward between the seats. "Is it what killed Jack Wagner? The flowers?"

"I don't know that either," she said.

"You didn't get anything out of it?"

"All I know is whoever wrote it can't spell."

I took the paper back from Mac and let my eyes scan the poem again. "Oh yeah, I see." I passed the note back over the seat and sat back. "Does that mean something?"

"Just that whoever wrote it could use a dictionary."

Abby L. Vandiver

Chapter Six

I'd never known Miss Vivee not to be able to just look at a body that had succumbed under suspicious circumstances and not know what killed it. It bothered me that she hadn't been able to do that for Jack Wagner. And from how quiet she'd kept on the ride home, I could tell that it bothered her, too.

Hazel Cobb talked all the way back to Yasamee, about a forty minute drive from the fairgrounds at Lincoln Park. Her chattering was exasperating to me after the long and harrowing day I had just lived through. So, I was happier than a tick on a fat dog, as Miss Vivee would say, when I saw the large, white gazebo sitting in the midst of the manicured green lawn that marked the center of town, letting me know we'd made it home.

I chuckled to myself at how sometimes I felt like I was turning into Miss Vivee. She had definitely invaded my spirit, and I found myself more like her all the time. I had taken to calling people by two names, just like her. And I was spitting out her southern colloquialisms so often, people would

44

probably have a hard time knowing that I had been a northerner all my life.

We crossed the center of town that was flanked on four sides by the town's main buildings – library, Baptist church, the movie theater, and Jellybean's Café and headed down Magnolia to Mac's house.

Yasamee, a small coastal city off the Savannah River, was a quiet and idyllic place. Everyone neighbors – they knew each other's name, and for the most part, all of their business. It was a place from a different time – a time more simple and unhurried, and except for all the murders I'd encountered since I arrived, it was a storybook kind of town.

After we dropped Mac off, we re-crossed the square to get to Piedmont Avenue where the bed and breakfast was located. As we drove down the street, I felt the stress of the day dissipate. I was glad to call this place home. My mother, I knew, didn't like that I had settled down there.

At my age, even with small children and a husband, my mother, Justin Dickerson, Biblical archaeologist extraordinaire, had travelled the world participating in digs in Jerusalem, Turkey, and Egypt, she had even excavated all over the United States. She wanted the same for me and wished I spent less time at the Maypop and more time on digs. She had yet to meet Miss Vivee, and would be really surprised at my choice of company, considering Miss Vivee's age and the penchant she had for attracting murders. I had been her cohort in solving more than a couple of them.

Yes. Murders in Yasamee had certainly become the fare of the day. And one thing for sure, if I'd learned anything from hanging out with Miss Vivee, it was that murder followed her around like a love-struck puppy.

I had come to Yasamee to hide out from the FBI, and it was on the second day after I arrived that Gemma Burke was murdered, bringing the FBI right to me. I had jumped "out of the frying pan right into the fire," as Miss Vivee would say. But coming to Yasamee had also given me Bay.

We pulled up in the driveway at the Maypop and I helped Miss Vivee and Cat out of the car.

Maypop, the edible fruit part of the North American passion flower, was perfect for the name of the house. It was an enormous colonial painted a bright white, and had black shutters that framed an abundance of windows across its front. The brick walkway was bordered with pink azalea bushes, and the lush glossy foliage and exotic colored blooms of the magenta begonias. The steps led up to a wide, airy, wrap-around porch. It was inviting at first sight.

I let out a pent up breath as soon as I stuck the key in the lock of the double oak door.

I had originally planned on going back home to Cleveland, stay there while I looked for another dig site – do all the things my mother wanted me to do, but it just hadn't worked out like that. I had become part of the Pennywell-Colquett family. For better or worse. I remembered the disappointment in my mother's voice, how she had just grunted and moved on to another subject when I told her I hadn't given up on my career, but I wasn't planning on leaving Georgia any time soon.

I unlocked the door, and stood back while Miss Vivee and Cat came in. Without stopping, she came in the front door and went out the back. She said she wanted to check on her greenhouse. She seemed troubled and unusually bemused. I asked her if she wanted me to help her, she told me she didn't need help to water flowers.

Well, she isn't too upset not to be rude.

I didn't argue, and took it that she wanted to work on that note. I left her to herself. I knew Renmar and Brie wouldn't be long coming back, they'd check on her then.

I went upstairs and took the first look at myself since the fair fiasco in the cheval mirror in my room. I did look a mess. Renmar was right. I hoped Bay hadn't had the same reaction to my appearance as she had.

I peeled my clothes off, threw them into the hamper and hit the shower. I turned on the water and made it as hot as I could stand. I wanted to wash all the madness – and death – away.

I poured shampoo into my hand, massaged it into my hair, and started thinking about that note and all those people that had gotten sick.

What in the world is going on?

I squirted some conditioner in my hand and slathered it on, pulling the creamy liquid down the length of my hair. "Was someone trying to kill all those people at the fair?" I said aloud.

What would have happened if I had eaten that pie?

A chill ran down my spine.

And then to make their murderous intentions into a game?

Miss Vivee was right, that was the action of someone with a sick mind. But Miss Vivee, even before anyone else thought about it, wouldn't give in to it. She refused to play along. I smiled. Kudos to her for that.

I lathered up my loofah, and thought about Camren Wagner. In a way, she reminded me of Renmar – the beautiful clear skin, the ever present winning smile, and that conspicuous Southern drawl. And maybe, I supposed, how she had carried on after the death of her husband, as if nothing had happened, were all part of that persona. The joviality and affability she exuded, all the while standing in front of an empty chair where her husband, who was now underneath a sheet dead, was supposed to be. I knew that no matter how much time I spent in the south, and picked up their mannerisms, I could never put on that kind of show if anything happened to Bay.

I rinsed off and stepped out of the shower. I grabbed a towel and dried off. I leaned forward over the sink and stared at my reflection in the medicine chest mirror. I turned from side to side, stroked my chin and forehead with my fingers, and thought that I didn't look so much like me anymore. I was changing – growing. I guess. I wasn't really sure. I let out a long sigh.

Turning from the mirror, I grabbed the bottle of Nivea and sat down on the side of the bed. Rubbing the lotion slowly over my body I thought about my life now.

I hadn't really given up on my career, even if my mother thought I had. Since I'd been in Georgia, I had excavated a four-thousand year old Native American site on Stallings Island. I was the first that had been given permission to do so in more than seventy-five years. And even though it was because of my mother's clout that I'd gotten the job, I had done really well there. I was the one who discovered Renmar's fish, swimming in an interior waterway for thousands of years. It had been an invaluable find. And that little unearthing had raised my clout tenfold in the world of ichthyology, and even a few with the Archaeology Conservancy, the AMA or ABA of my profession. Either way it was all good for my career. And the only down side had been Gemma Burke keeling over dead in a bowl of Renmar's pseudo-extinct fish stew, and Oliver Gibbons sprawled out across the sand shoal leading to the island poisoned with the nicotine from his e-cigarettes.

And then there was Rock Trap Gap.

I initially broke into the place, a federally guarded archaeological site, after I had visited it with my mother. We'd gone to prove my theory that the Maya once lived in the United States, specifically northern Georgia. I left there running like a fugitive, but after showing what a good archaeologist I was at Stallings Island, the Conservancy had given me permission to excavate there. That find would have been the career defining moment for me. Unfortunately, I was unable to even get a foothold in proving my supposition of the American-Maya connection because another body showed up. And before it was over, the body count had risen to two.

I put the lotion bottle up, turned the light off and climbed into bed. I closed my eyes, happy to be away from all the madness of the day. My thoughts drifted to Bay and I sighed a smile.

Then my eyes popped open.

Wait! Death didn't follow Miss Vivee around like a love sick puppy. It shadowed me.

Before I even came to Yasamee, my manager on my dig in Belize, Jairo Zacapa died. Shot. Second day in Yasamee there was Gemma Burke. Dry Drowned. Stallings Island and Oliver Gibbons. Poisoned. Rock Trap Gap, and Aaron Coulter and Laura Tyler . . .

Murdered. All of them murdered.

I sat straight up in bed.

Oh. My. God.

I was a homicide magnet.

Chapter Seven

I came down the oak staircase into the foyer and caught a whiff of something scrumptious wafting out from the kitchen.

"Here I come," I said out loud as my stomach growled in synchronous response. I hadn't eaten anything at the fair the day before after all the uproar of people getting sick. And I was starving. I couldn't wait to see what delicious dish Renmar had whipped up for the Monday morning crowd.

The dining room to the left of the foyer was full. Even more than usual. I guess word had gotten around of all the blue ribbons Renmar had swept up at the fair. I waved at the people in the dining area as I followed my nose toward the kitchen. With my thoughts wrapped around food, I must have missed the creaking of the closet door under the staircase when it opened.

I let out a screech as something reached out and yanked me in. I stumbled and bumped my head on the sloping ceiling.

"Oh crap!"

Bay put a finger up to his mouth to shush me, then reached up and pulled the chain, turning off the light.

"What the hey?" I said and tried to adjust my eyes to the dark.

"You got away from me last night."

I chuckled. "No. You got away from me. Seems like your job is your favorite girl, and, as your grandmother would say, I'm just playing second fiddle."

He clicked on the light. "Did my grandmother tell you that? You don't really think that, do you?" Brows knitted in slight confusion, his eyes narrowed so much that with his thick, dark eyelashes they appeared closed. "I try not to let work get in the way of us."

I wanted to keep up the ruse, I enjoyed him being so concerned about me. But he was smelling so good, and looking so cute, I just couldn't do it.

"Just kidding," I said and punched him. "Sheesh!"

"Oh," he said and clicked the light back off. "Good, then give me a kiss." I could feel his hot breath on my face and I instinctively raised my head and closed my eyes.

"So, are you going to marry me?" he asked.

"I thought we were going to kiss?" I said. "What's with all the talking?"

"No," he said and pulled back. "No kisses for you. Not until you answer my question."

"I don't think that's legal."

"What?"

"Pulling a girl into a tight, dark closet, offering her kisses, then not delivering."

"I'm the law in this closet," Bay said. "And I say it's perfectly legal. And don't try to get off the subject here. Are you going to marry me or not?"

"Are you going to kiss me or not?"

"Only if you're going to marry me."

"Then get to kissing," I said and reached up and pecked him somewhere on his face.

"Is that a yes?" he asked.

"Yes. I guess so. But, what happened to a romantic expensive restaurant, down on one-knee, you-complete-me, prepared speech kind of proposal?"

"What? You don't like the closet?"

"I love the closet," I said. "And I love you. Now give me my ring." I poked him in his stomach.

"Not yet. I have to ask your father, get his blessing. You know I'm a southern gentleman."

"Then why you keep wanting an answer from me now?"

"Because I needed to get your dad's phone number." He clicked on the light.

"Omigosh!" I said and laughed. I blinked trying to get used to the change in lighting. "You're the FBI, and you can't get a phone number?"

"Can you just text it to me?" he asked. "Please."

My stomach rumbled.

"What was that?" he asked.

"I'm hungry and you're keeping me from whatever your mother has smelling so good in the kitchen." I put my hand on the knob of the door. "I'll text you my dad's number, but you better speak to my mom, too. She runs things at our house."

"And for some reason, I'm betting you think you're going to be doing the same thing at our house."

"Not if you keep food from me, like you're doing now. I'll be too weak to try and run anything."

He leaned down and gave me a kiss. "I'll keep you fed and happy when we get married."

"And let me run everything?"

"Everything," he said. "I promise."

He gave me a real kiss that time, and then not only was my stomach growling, but my head was reeling, and my knees went weak.

Mmmmm . . . I'm already happy.

"I can't wait for you to be my bride." Bay said, pulling his lips away from mine. "You *are* my world, you know? Prepared speech aside."

I smiled. "And I can't wait to get that *two-carat* ring." I pulled my cell phone from my pocket and texted him my parents' numbers.

He chuckled. "Two carats. Right." We heard the ding of his phone, letting us know there was a message received. "Okay," he said and kissed me again. "So, look. I gotta make a phone call," he said. "Then I have to go up to Augusta to the coroner's office to check on Jackson Wagner's autopsy results."

"They finished with the autopsy?" I asked. "That was quick, especially for a Sunday.'

"Just the preliminary report. Toxicology is still out, but the ME hinted that he had some pertinent info for me."

"Oh, okay."

"So, go get something to eat, and I'll come say bye after I make my call."

He leaned down and gave me a peck on the lips.

I made it into the kitchen, a grin on my face wide as the Savannah, thoughts of marrying Bay on my mind. "Mornin,'" I said.

Brie, Hazel Cobb and Renmar were talking – gossiping – about the fair, and the entries into the cook-off. Brie and Hazel sat at the large kitchen table drinking coffee. Renmar stood on the other side of the oversized, butcher block topped island stacking plates and carrying them over to the sink.

The large chef's kitchen was bright, shiny and cheery. A big window over the farmhouse sink let in lots of natural light, and bright white eyelet cotton curtains were ruffled by the breeze that blew in.

I walked across the rust and black checkerboard cork floor, my feet sinking into it as I made my way to the six burner aluminum gas stove. There, sat atop of it, were homemade cinnamon buns topped with glazed pecans in a glass Pyrex dish

Oh my . . .

My mouth watered as I plucked a butter knife from the silverware drawer, bumped it shut with my

Abby L. Vandiver

hip, and pulled a small plate from the cabinet. I cut out one of the gooey rolls, and slid it onto the plate, then licked the knife, and my fingers. I grabbed a glass, and went to the fridge and poured myself some milk, then slid into a seat at the table with Brie and Hazel Cobb. I broke off a huge piece of the pastry and stuffed it into my mouth.

I chewed slowly to savor every morsel, my eyes almost shutting. I watched Renmar through half-closed eyes as she squirted dish liquid on the plates in the sink, steam rising as she sprayed them with hot water.

I plucked off another piece, plopped it into my mouth and licked my fingers.

"Why would you have my mother grow dreadlocks?" Renmar said, just out of blue. She had turned from the sink, her hands covered in the sudsy water.

I turned to look in back of me to see who she was talking to. Had someone just walked in? No. No one was behind me. I looked at Brie and Hazel Cobb, who were looking at me.

"I'm talking to you, Miss Logan," Renmar said wiping her hands on a dishtowel, her accent more pronounced than usual.

My eyes got wide, and a pecan got stuck in my throat. "Me?" came my choked response.

"Yes. You." She placed her hands on her hips. "She doesn't need any help going down the crazy road."

56

"I . . ." I opened my mouth to answer and then shut it again. I didn't know what to say because there was no telling what Miss Vivee had told her.

There was an awkward silence as everyone waited for me to answer.

"Morning." Bay walked into the doorway and stopped. Licking his thick lips, he rubbed his hands together, and smiled wide, showing a mouth full of white teeth.

Saved by the bell – or rather Bay.

Thank you, husband-to-be.

"My, my," he said. "I've never seen so many beautiful women in one place in all my life."

"Hi Bay," Hazel said smiling.

"Good morning," Brie greeted him.

He walked around the table and kissed Hazel Cobb.

"Give me a hug," she said.

He did and then kissed his Auntie Brie. He went over to his mother, who still stood by the sink, and gave her a big bear hug.

"My favorite son," Renmar said.

"Your only son, Ma." He planted a big kiss on her forehead, each cheek, and then touched her nose with his finger tip. "And the luckiest son in the world."

His gestures and words made her eyes gleam with joy. She wasn't thinking about anything I'd done anymore.

Thank goodness.

"What you got in here smelling so good?" Bay asked his mother. He went over and sniffed around the stove. "What's in here?" He put his hand on the handle of one of the double ovens built into the wall.

"Don't you dare!" Renmar said. "I've got a cake in there."

"Mmmm," he said. "I've got business in Augusta, but I'll be back to get some of that this afternoon." He rubbed his stomach. "Save me a piece?"

"I can't promise," Renmar said. "You know how people love my red velvet cake."

"Red velvet?" Bay said, a grin spreading across his face. "Now, Ma, you know I have to have a piece of that. I thought I was your favorite son?"

Renmar chuckled. "I'll see what I can do."

"Okay, I gotta go," he said. He came over, bent down and kissed me on my cheek.

"I thought maybe you hadn't seen Logan sitting there," Hazel Cobb said. "You hadn't said a word to her, like you forgot about her."

"Never," he said and winked at me. "I'll be back." He waved a good-bye and left.

"One thing about Logan being here," Brie said. "We get to see Bay more often."

"Yeah, that's true," Hazel Cobb said. "We also get to go to more funerals."

"Hazel," Brie said. "That's not a nice thing to say." She looked at me and rubbed my arm.

"May not be nice, Brie," Hazel responded, "But it's true."

"Hazel," Renmar warned.

Oh now she's taking up for me?

Hazel chuckled. "Bless her heart, ever since Logan came, murder is a common occurrence in Yasamee."

Seems to me that I've learned since I've been here that "bless her heart" isn't a nice thing to say about someone.

"It's true." Brie bit back a laugh. "And Momma has been off the chain."

"Off the chain?" Hazel said and busted out laughing.

I didn't see anything funny.

Ever since I came, Renmar and Brie had just thrown up their hands when it came to Miss Vivee. And they mostly blamed me. Reminding me that Miss Vivee hadn't left the house for twenty years until I arrived.

And, they noted, it was after I arrived that the murders started. I didn't need them telling me that, I had had that epiphany the night before.

I stuffed the last piece of pecan roll in my mouth. I wanted to make a quick exit.

"Logan you need to go out there and see about her," Renmar said as I sat my dish, silverware, and glass in the sink. "She's been wandering around all morning in that backyard. Her and that dog." She glanced out the kitchen window. "Those are the same clothes she had on yesterday, I do believe, and her hair, even if she is trying a new hairdo, looks unkempt."

Why does she always relegate me that duty?

"I'm worried about her," Brie said.

Renmar looked at me. "You're the only one that can talk to her. She doesn't listen to anything I have to say, even when she's . . ." She looked out the window again "Even when she's not feeling disoriented."

Didn't Renmar just accuse me of helping her go down the crazy road?

I followed Renmar's eyes out the window and it made my heart skip a beat. I immediately felt bad. Miss Vivee did look lost. She was walking through her flower garden, it seemed, in a daze. Even Cat had her head hung low.

"I think she's okay," I said. Although I wasn't too sure, I'd never seen Miss Vivee look like that.

"I hope you're right," Renmar said. "I'm thinking about making an appointment with a doctor up in Augusta one of our guests this morning told me about. She specializes in the elderly."

That thought choked me up.

I glanced back out of the window. "I'll go and talk to her," I said.

"You know," Brie said. "If something has gone wrong with Momma's mind, there's no coming back from it. It's the way she'll be from here on out."

"Oh Brie," Renmar said her face frowning up. "You say the most God-awful things. That's your mother you're talking about. Don't go speaking it into the atmosphere that she's gone bonkers."

Isn't what Brie said the same thing she espoused?

I pushed open the old wooden screen door that led to the huge backyard from the kitchen. As soon as I stepped outside my senses were invaded with the smell of wildflowers, jasmine and honeysuckle; the bright, vibrant pinks, reds, yellows and purples of the delicate flowers; and the chirping of the birds that filled Miss Vivee's garden.

I watched Miss Vivee as I approached. Her long white hair was hanging loose, it was disheveled, and looked as if she had been twisting it with her fingers. And she looked, I don't know . . . Confused? Befuddled?

Hadn't she just been okay yesterday? Could something like that happen so overnight?

Cat walked over to me and I reached down to pet her. Brie was right, though. There was no going back. With all the research and support, there was no cure for dementia. I stood up and stared at Miss Vivee, zooming in on her face and then to her eyes.

"Why are you looking at me all crazy," she said.

"Me? I'm not looking crazy?" I shook my head and swallowed.

Should I tell her it was she that had the crazy look?

"What's wrong with you?" I said instead.

She furrowed her brow. "Why? What do you know?"

"Know?" I asked. "About what?"

"Never mind," she waved her hand at me.

"What's wrong with your hair?" I thought I'd try a different approach.

"My hair?" she reached up and tucked a few stray strands behind her ear, then patted it down. "What's wrong with it?"

"Well, it looks unkempt. And you told Renmar I was having you grow dreadlocks."

"Unkempt?" She grinned. "You're starting to sound like an old woman."

"It's what Renmar said. I just used her words. But don't get away from this dreadlock thing."

"She was bothering me about my hair. So I told her it was your fault my hair looks like this. She won't try and put you away if you're acting a little crazy."

"Is that what you think? That you're acting a little crazy?"

"Hell no!" she said her voice a little louder than usual. Cat let out a yelp, I guessed dittoing the sentiment. "Anyway, crazy people don't know they're crazy, so, it wouldn't make any sense to get my opinion about it. But it's none of her business if I comb my hair or not."

"Why wouldn't you comb your hair?"

"I didn't *not* comb it on purpose. I was up really late talking to Mac," she said and looked off as if she was remembering the conversation. "It was probably close to ten before I got to bed."

"10pm?"

"Of course, 10pm. Good lord, what other time could I be talking about?"

I didn't know, but ten didn't seem late to me.

"How does that have anything to do with your hair?" I said instead.

"Well. After we talked, I just tossed and turned and couldn't get any sleep. I probably was pulling on it all night. Do I have bags under my eyes?"

She pushed her face close to mine and blinked her eyes hard several times.

I pulled back and tried to examine them. Maybe there were some bags under there, but there were so many wrinkles, who could tell?

"I don't see any," I said. I got back on the subject at hand. "What were you and Mac talking about?"

"How we'd be able to prove my innocence."

"Your innocence?"

"Yeah."

"Innocence of what?"

"Murder," she said.

Chapter Eight

Now I was really getting nervous. I remembered how people thought Miss Vivee had something to do with Bay's father's death. She had explained to me that he was suffering from cancer, and had requested her help to end his pain. Such actions are legal now in a few places, but I'm sure they weren't legal anywhere when Louis Colquett passed away. They were very close, Bay had explained to me, and whether it was true or not, he said, no one blamed her. But to me, it just exemplified who she was – brave and willing to go to the end to help a friend.

But now, I wondered, *do I need to get worried?*

"Whose murder?" I asked.

"Jack Wagner's murder," Miss Vivee said. "Who else?"

I furrowed my brow. "Why would anyone think you murdered him? You didn't even know him, did you?"

"No. And -"

"And," I took over talking and didn't let her finish. "We don't know for sure that he was murdered."

"Everyone, but you it seems," she nodded her head toward me, "knows the man was murdered. Even the Sheriff said it."

"I'll wait for the coroner's report," I said. "Because frankly I've had enough of murder."

"Have you now?" She looked at me with a devilish smirk.

"What is this thing you have with murder, Miss Vivee?" I said. "I mean, I know I've run into a couple on my own, but you just seem to attract them."

"I attract them?"

"Yes, you," I said, trying to project my thoughts of being a murder magnet onto her. "You attract them."

"Like a moth to a flame?" She let her gaze drift.

"Yeah," I said. "Like a moth to a flame."

"I knew you'd come, you know" Miss Vivee said after a short pause.

"Knew I'd come where?" I asked. "Out back?"

"No. To Yasamee," she said and walked off toward her greenhouse. Cat followed behind her.

To Yasamee? I mouthed under my breath and followed her. She passed the miniature putt-putt golf course, and on to the other side of her greenhouse. She sat on a wrought iron bench, the black paint peeling, showing years of wear. I'd never known her to sit out here. I sat down next to her, and so did Cat.

"How do you feel, Miss Vivee?" I asked. I began thinking that maybe a trip to Augusta to see that geriatric doctor was a good idea.

"How am I supposed to feel?" she asked.

"I mean . . ." I licked my lips, and blinked my eyes. I didn't want to say anything to upset her. "You should feel however you feel." I looked at her. "Good." I said and nodded my head reassuringly. "You should feel good."

"How do *you* feel?" she said and raised an eyebrow.

"I feel good," I said. I patted her on her knee like she often does to me. "I'm feeling really good."

"Well, you're acting awfully daffy."

Time to change the subject. Again. "How did you know I'd come to Yasamee?"

"It was my destiny. Our destiny."

I raised an eyebrow. *Okay.* I thought. This was getting wackier by the minute.

"Our destiny?"

"Yes," she said." I had prepared for it. And the wave of murder that came with you."

Oh. My. God. She is going crazy.

I furrowed my brow and narrowed my eyes. "Now wait a minute . . ."

"Gemma Burke's murder wasn't the first – or second – one I'd seen." Looking down at her hands, she smoothed out the wrinkles, pausing to rub one of the larger of the many dark spots on it. "I'd been told that all of this was my destiny. I just didn't know I'd be so old when it happened. When you came."

Now she was scaring me. And even though I had kind of come to that realization the night before, I definitely wasn't prepared to hear her tell me it was divine providence.

"All of what, Miss Vivee?"

"The murders." She locked her eyes with mine. "Solving the murders."

"Anyway," I said, not wanting to talk about that anymore. "What makes you and Mac think that you'd be a suspect in Jack Wagner's, uhm, death?"

"The note," she said and nothing more.

I paused and thought about what was written on the note. I couldn't remember Miss Vivee being mentioned, although honestly, I didn't remember much about what it said at all.

"What about the note?" I finally asked.

"The flowers."

"Yeah. What about the flowers?"

Spit it out, Miss Vivee.

"I have them."

I hadn't the faintest idea what that meant. "Oh, Miss Vivee, just tell me." I voiced my impatience. "What are you talking about?"

"I have every flower on the note."

"*You* have?"

"Yes. In my garden. In my greenhouse. I have each one of those flowers."

"So?"

"So they don't just grow, all of them, at the same place. I had to plant them." She was waving her hands around, raising her voice.

"Lots of people have gardens," I said letting my voice get a little louder, too. "What's the big deal?"

"Big deal?" She let her hands drop as if they had gone limp. "Sometimes, girl, I think you ain't as smart as all your college degrees let on you are." She shook her head. "All the plants on that list are poisonous."

"All of them?"

She turned and looked at me and made a face. "Didn't you read the note?"

"Yeah."

"Don't you remember it said deadly flowers?"

I didn't remember it saying that.

"No," I said. "I don't remember that." I shook my head vigorously, and let my eyes roll up and to the right to think about it. I looked back down at her. I didn't remember much but I was positive it didn't say "deadly flowers."

"And you have all those poisonous flowers? Here?"

"Yes."

I made a mental note not to touch any of Miss Vivee's flowers ever again.

I noticed the worry that seemed to nag her. "I honestly don't remember the words 'deadly flowers,' Miss Vivee, but I do remember it said 'field of flowers.' You remember that?"

She nodded as if she wasn't really listening.

"Miss Vivee." I grabbed her hand. I really wanted to try and ease her mind. "That's right, isn't it," I said. "Field of flowers was written on the note?"

"Yes," she said. "Twice."

"Right. And there's a whole bunch of flowers outside the tents. At the fairgrounds. Flowers were everywhere."

She nodded.

"You remember that?"

"Yes. I remember that."

"Maybe that's what it's talking about," I said. "You got the note at the fairgrounds. There are flowers at the fairgrounds. Maybe some of those flowers are on the list? We should check them out."

"No. Only one of them is there."

"How do you know?" I tilted my head and looked at her. "You couldn't have looked at them."

"I did. I saw them when we drove into Lincoln Park. Plus, I know that field like the back of my hand. That's where the last murder in Yasamee happened."

"The last murder in Yasamee was Oliver Gibbons," I said. "He died outside his beach house right down the road."

"Well, I mean the first murder." She held her hand up to stop me, I had just opened my mouth to correct her again. "Gemma Burke was the first one you were here for," she said anticipating what I was going to say. "But remember when she died I told you then that there hadn't been a murder in Yasamee in sixty-five years?"

"Not really."

Who could remember all those murders ago?

"Well, that's where they found the body," Miss Vivee said. "At the fairgrounds in Lincoln Park."

"You didn't have anything to do with that one, did you?"

She cut me a look. "No, and this one either."

"I don't know," I said teasing. "You do have all the flowers." I just wanted to lighten up her mood, and help dispel her sense of doom.

"That's why Mac was trying to help me clear my name. As soon as the investigators find out that Jack Wagner was poisoned by a flower on that list, and I'm the only one with those flowers, they'll come after me."

"Did he die from being poisoned by one of the flowers on that list?"

Miss Vivee let out a long sigh. "Why else would someone write that note?" She seemed more to be questioning that fact, than giving a definitive answer.

"Well, it doesn't matter. Bay is the investigator on that case," I said. "Your grandson wouldn't come after you, or arrest you. He loves you too much to do that."

"Do you think he would help me get away?" she asked, turning her whole body to me, a tiny sparkle appearing in her eye.

"Oh my goodness, Miss Vivee."

"Well, it wouldn't be the first time he let a fugitive get away." She looked at me out the side of her eye.

"I was not a fugitive."

"*Hmpf*," she said and turned back to sit facing forward. "Anyhoo," she continued. "I don't know of any other place that might have all the flowers on that list. Other than my place. And Bay would have to do his job, grandmother or not. So, Mac told me to gaggle it. See what I could find."

"Did you look it up?"

"How do you think I would have done that all by myself? You have to help me gaggle it."

"Google it. What do you want me to lookup?"

"Good Lord. Can't you keep up?" she scrunched her nose at me. "Another greenhouse that has all of the poisonous plants on the list."

I pulled out my phone and swiped across the front of it. "Do greenhouses list their plant inventory?" I glanced at her. "Do you list yours?"

"No. How would I list my inventory on there?" She pointed at my phone. "Can you write on it?"

I shook my head. "No. But if you did list it anywhere, at a registry, or somewhere, then they might publish it on their website."

She looked at me with an air of disdain. "I haven't the faintest idea what you are talking about."

"Let's look up plant farms," I said. No need trying to teach her anything about the last fifty years of technology. She still had a 1950s Westinghouse clock radio on the nightstand in her room. "Plant farms," I said typing it in. "Isn't that what they call places that sell flowers to florists?" I glanced over at her.

"Oh heavenly Father, Logan. Why in the world would a florist sell deadly flowers?" She blew out a breath. "You send flowers to people you care about, not ones you want to kill."

"Okay. Fine." I entered new search terms. "Here," I said. "Botanical gardens. How about that?" I asked. "A few greenhouses came up when I did a general search of 'flowers, greenhouses, farms' and they have a botanical garden." I looked at her. "Wouldn't people put poisonous flowers on display?"

"Yes. Now you're using that knocker of yours." She took her fist and tapped me on my head.

"Okay. Now let's see where the closest one is," I said reading the listings my Google search provided.

"Put in Freemont and Augusta County," Miss Vivee said wiggling her finger at my phone. "It'd have to have been somewhere close."

"I meant to ask you that, why do they call it the Freemont County Fair, when it's in Augusta County?"

"Long story," she said and pointed at my screen. "Type it in," she ordered. "Freemont and Augusta."

"I don't have to," I said. "Google knows where I am and gives me the closest ones."

"Well, don't that beat all?" She leaned in closer to my phone, nose nearly touching the screen and squinted her eyes. "A phone that knows where you are." She turned from the phone and looked up at me. "Will wonders never cease."

"Are you blind?" I said and pulled the phone away from her face. "Okay. Here's one." I clicked on the

link. "Krieger's Greenhouse and Botanical Gardens."
I scanned their home page.

"Do they have the flowers that were on the note?"
she asked.

"I don't know, but one of their collections is
named the Poison Garden."

"Bingo," Miss Vivee said, and hit me on my head
again.

Chapter Nine

We decided that I would drive us up to Krieger's Greenhouse so we could check out the flowers on display in their Poison Garden. It wouldn't be an exhaustive search to exonerate her as a suspect, I reasoned, but I figured that it would make her feel better to know she wasn't the only one that had the flowers on the note.

And Miss Vivee did seem to feel better after we made our plans. Then she took one look at herself and got even more energized.

"Come on," she said. "I have to make myself look presentable. I look a mess. Let's go Cat."

Cat jumped up, tail wagging and ran to the house and back three times before we got to it. I breathed a sigh of relief.

Maybe she'd taken a U-turn on that crazy road.

I followed Miss Vivee and walked back in through the screen door into the kitchen. She went and stood in the middle of the floor and flapped a hand at Renmar. "Well, I guess you finally got your way," she said.

"What are you talking about, Mother?" Renmar asked. She glanced up at me from icing the red velvet cake she had been baking earlier as if to ask if everything was okay.

I didn't let on to anything.

Actually, I don't have a clue about anything Miss Vivee is up to.

"Logan's gonna take me to that old folks' senility doctor up in Augusta that you wanted me to go to."

I am? First I'd heard of it.

"Mother!" Renmar said and laid down her buttercream covered spatula. "I'd never-"

"Don't deny it, Renmar. You've been trying to get me certified crazy ever since I turned a hundred."

"You're not a hundred, Mother," Renmar said.

"Momma," Brie said. "Don't nobody mean no harm. We only want you to be happy and healthy."

"I'd be happy if the two of you would leave me alone. And," Miss Vivee nodded her head and lifted an eyebrow. "I'm more than a hundred, and healthier than the both of you to boot." She ran her eyes up and down each one then kept them on Brie. "And you," she pointed a finger. "You could stand to lose a few pounds."

"That's exactly why we wanted you to go and see someone," Renmar said. "You've got no filter."

"Filter?" Miss Vivee said. "Oh, so you do admit to wanting me to go to the crazy doctor?"

"No," Renmar said sheepishly, and went back to icing her cake.

"When you get to be my age," Miss Vivee said. "You can say what you wanna say. Don't need a filter. But it don't make me no never mind, no how. Logan's gonna take me up there. Give you what you want."

"I can take you, Mother," Renmar offered.

"I don't want you to take me," Miss Vivee said. "Logan'll take me and I won't have to hear a whole bunch of talking about it. Isn't that right, Logan?"

Everyone looked at me. I couldn't let Miss Vivee down in front of everyone even though I knew she was telling one of her tall tales. We hadn't planned on going anywhere near any doctor's office. I had spoken to Renmar directly about the geriatric physician and didn't even know her name. I didn't know how Miss Vivee knew.

"Yes ma'am," I said. "Not a word from me." I pretended to lock my lips and throw away the key.

"When are you going, Momma?" Brie asked.

"Right now," Miss Vivee said. "We're going right now."

"You have an appointment *now*?" Renmar looked at us suspiciously.

I let my eyes wander over to the refrigerator and kept them there.

"Yes. I do," Miss Vivee said.

"I still don't know how you knew about that doctor." Renmar narrowed her eyes. "And, how did you get an appointment so quickly?" she asked.

"I know people, and people know me," Miss Vivee said. "Wasn't hard at all. Was it, Logan?"

I really wish she wouldn't drag me into her lies.

"No," I shook my head, eyes wide. "Wasn't hard at all." I didn't know how Miss Vivee thought she'd fake a trip to the doctor, but I was committed – I was going to go down with the ship.

Renmar waved her fingers up and down Miss Vivee, just as she had done me. "You do plan on putting on some fresh street clothes, and combing your hair, don't you?"

"Of course I'm going to comb my hair," Miss Vivee said. "I already told you dreadlocks wasn't my idea. I was just going along with this makeover Logan wanted to give me."

Renmar cut her eyes at me.

"But it's just too much." Miss Vivee continued. She tried to run her bony fingers through her hair, but caught them on a tangle. "Ouch!" Miss Vivee said and shook her head. "Plus, it hurts."

"Well, now at least *you're* showing an inkling of some sense," Renmar said. "And I'll have a talk with you, Miss Logan, as soon as the two of you get back."

Oh crap.

Abby L. Vandiver

Chapter Ten

I pushed Miss Vivee into my jeep after fighting with her for ten minutes about Cat coming along. I was afraid her little dog would relieve herself on a prized flower. Miss Vivee insisted that it would be good for the soil.

"So," I said after I got in and buckled up, "What is this thing about the doctor?"

"I heard Renmar talking about it this morning," Miss Vivee said. "How she thought she could keep a secret by discussing it in the dining room with all the guests there is a mystery to me."

"I still don't understand."

"I found out the name of that doctor, and I want you to drive me by there."

"They're not going to see you today," I told her. "Doctor's offices are busy, they don't do walk-ins."

"What do you think? You're talking to a child? I know that they're busy."

"So what's the plan?" I may as well cut to chase.

"You'll take me by the office, I'll make an appointment for another day, and they'll give me an appointment card. I'll show that to Renmar." She held out her hand like it was all so simple and easy to see. "And even though I didn't see the doctor, it'll prove I was there today. Renmar'll be none the wiser."

How does she think of these things?

"Where is this doctor?"

"How am I supposed to know?" Miss Vivee scowled. "I know her name, you'll have to gaggle where she is."

"Google. And you better hope she's in her office today."

"I think you're the one that better hope she's there," she said, she shifted her shoulders back and sat up straight, her eyebrows lifted. "Otherwise, Renmar'll think you're a liar."

"Me?"

"Yeah, she already thinks I'm senile." A smiled curled up her lip. "She won't blame me."

Certainly not a way to start off a relationship with my future mother-in-law.

Luckily for me the doctor was in. She was located in Augusta not too far from our exit for the Krieger Greenhouse off I-520 next to Doctor's Hospital. The office staff seemed quite comfortable with Miss Vivee and her tall tales, and accommodated her without any trouble. I guess they were used to her kind. They took her in the back, and instructed me to stay put. Fifteen minutes later with appointment card tucked carefully in her purse, she came back out laughing with the nurses and we headed out to the greenhouse.

"I thought it was a botanical garden," Miss Vivee said as we drove up to the spot my Google Earth had led us to. She looked at me. "It's an arboretum."

And that was exactly what the sign read. Krieger Arboretum. No mention of a garden, let alone a poison garden.

"I thought so, too," I said. I pulled the car over, put it in park, and rechecked the GPS on my iPhone. I checked the directions and looked back up at the sign. "We're in the right place."

I put the car back in drive and headed in. The road into the arboretum must have gone on for a nearly three quarters of a mile and was banked by an archway made up of maple trees. The trees that hovered over the wide concrete road had to be decades old. They had smooth, silvery gray bark and a crown spreading out over the road with masses of green leaves that shaded the road so much so that only streaks of sunlight were able to push through.

As we went down the road, I could hear the birds twittering and smell the crisp, fresh air breezing around us. Once past the trees we came upon a clearing. And there was the most beautiful courtyard I'd ever seen.

A cascading waterfall fountain set in the center, it was made up of blue-green, yellow and orange glazed tiles that glistened in the sun. The fountain was surrounded by colorful, fragrant flowers, all in full bloom with butterflies flitting about. Cobblestone pavers led to an English cottage-like structure complete with ivy growing up the front, and an asymmetrical composition of small trees, shrubs and tall grass bordering it. It was magical.

The sign in front of the small structure read "Office."

I wouldn't mind coming to work here every day, I thought.

I stopped to take it all in, and noticed how Miss Vivee was shifting around in her seat. Her eyes gleamed, she tapped her feet, and had clasped her hand together.

"Isn't it just breathtaking?" she said and smiled so wide I thought her dentures would fall out.

In front of stone structure were signs, one pointing left that read, "Botanical Gardens," and one pointing right that said, "Arboretum."

"Botanical Gardens?" I asked.

"No," Miss Vivee said and glanced at me. "We need to speak to someone. The Office would be the best place to start."

"Okay," I said and parked the car. She rarely let me in on her game plan when searching for clues, but that was okay because I believed that Miss Vivee herself didn't know her plan of action going in. She'd just wing it.

As I opened Miss Vivee's door to help her out of the car, I saw a man in my periphery walk toward us.

"Hello," he said.

Leaving Miss Vivee in her seat, I turned with a smile to greet the man. My facial expression quickly changed to surprise. "I know you," I said. It was the Official Guy from the fair. I couldn't remember his name.

"Gavin Tanner," Miss Vivee said.

I turned and looked at her and back at him. "That's right. Gavin."

He grinned and looked at Miss Vivee. "You remembered?"

Miss Vivee had a memory like a steel trap. I don't know why I let Renmar convince me that something was wrong with her brain.

"Of course I remember," Miss Vivee said. "Why wouldn't I?"

"I thought that was you I saw getting out of the truck," Gavin said. He walked over to the car, reached over me to help Miss Vivee out of the car.

"Hi, Mrs. Pennywell." He greeted her formally and took her hand. He held on to her long after she'd landed safely on the ground. "Fancy meeting you here."

"What are you doing here?" she asked, I think she was thrown off seeing him there, too, but she was a master at keeping a straight face.

"I work here," he said. "I was just helping out at the fair as part of my job?"

"Your job?"

"Yep. I work in Visitor Services, and sometimes I help out in the Horticulture Department."

"So then you knew about all those plants?"

"What plants?"

"On the note," Miss Vivee said. She looked at him suspiciously.

"On the note?" he asked his face scrunched. Then it seemed to dawn on him. "Oh no. I didn't read that note. I just ran it over to you." He stuck his hands in his pockets. Took them back out and put them behind his back. "There were plants on the note?" He stumbled over his words. "That's what made everybody sick? Plants?"

"You brought it all the way over to me and didn't read it?" Miss Vivee asked. I saw a small smirk cross her face.

"Yeah. Well." He ran his hair through his mop of curly black hair. "The fair director just told me to find you. You know, because that Sheriff said you could help." He scratched the back of his neck, then his elbow. "So that's what I did."

"And I gave you all that trouble."

"It wasn't really you, Mrs. Pennywell." He glanced over at me.

Wasn't me either, I started to say. *I tried to help.*

"No. You're right," she said. "It was my daughters."

He laughed and cracked his knuckles. "They were not letting me get anywhere near you. So . . ." He looked all around as if he was searching for something. "Did you get it figured out?"

"What?" Miss Vivee asked as if she didn't know what they were talking about.

"The note. The flowers on it. What did it all mean?"

"Oh yes, I did figure it out," she said. "They didn't mean anything."

"They didn't?" he smiled. Seemed like that was happy news to him.

"Yes," Miss Vivee said lowering her voice and leaning in to him. "I think it was food poisoning."

"Food poisoning?" He seemed to really get a kick out of that, he reeled back and let out a laugh. "Well, that's a good thing. It'd be an awful thing if Mr. Wagner died from something that he loved so much. That would have been ironic, huh?"

"He loved flowers?"

"Oh yeah," he said and then paused and looked at the two of us. "Oh. I guess you didn't know. This is his place." He spread out his arms. "Krieger Arboretum and Gardens."

"You don't say," Miss Vivee said.

"Well, you know, Mrs. Wagner owns it too – with her husband. Well when he was alive, I mean. But it's named after his mother. Mr. Wagner's mother. Krieger was her maiden name."

"His wife?" I asked. I remembered her from the fair. Dead husband laying on the ground not twenty feet away, and she acting as if she didn't have a care in the world. "What's her name?"

"Camren Wagner," he said.

"So now she owns this place?" Miss Vivee asked.

"Yeah. Well." He blew out a breath. "I guess so. You know, now that he's dead." More fidgeting. "Now that Mr. Wagner's dead." He coughed into his hand. "Anyway, we all figured the arboretum would be closed today. You know, with his death. A day of mourning, or something. But we're open and she's here." He clapped his hands and rubbed them together. "We're all here."

"Where is Mrs. Wagner now?" Miss Vivee asked.

"Where she always is. In her gardens."

"I can't believe she came to work today." I said, mumbling.

I don't know why though, I thought. *She didn't miss a beat when he died. The show must go on.*

"That's really strange," Miss Vivee said.

"Well, I guess it's no love lost between them," he ran his hand through his hair again, then pushed his hand down in his pockets."

"No love lost?"

"I think they were getting a divorce," he leaned in and spoke in a low voice. "She'd kind of already moved on."

"So you say she's here? In her gardens?" Miss Vivee asked turning around looking the way the arrow pointed. I thought sure she'd try to pry more information about a possible affair out of Gavin, but she didn't. "I thought this was an arboretum," she said instead.

"Oh yeah. It is," he said. "In a narrow sense an arboretum is a collection of trees, but today, when speaking of an arboretum it usually refers to a botanical garden. And our gardens are huge." He was right in his element talking about the place. "Still we have collections of *saliceta* and *querceta*, which are willows and oaks. Also magnolias. *Magnoliaceae* is the scientific name." He shook his head and grinned, his eyes big. "We have a lot of magnolia trees. But our main focus in the arboretum is in pomology."

"The cultivation of fruit trees?" Miss Vivee asked.

"Yes," Gavin Tanner smiled. It seemed to excite him for her to know what that meant. "When we're in full bloom," he started counting on his fingers. "We'll have blackberry, Pomegranate, pear, apple, peach, plum, fig, nectarine, pecan, Asian pear, fig and Japanese persimmon trees." He swallowed hard and took in a breath as if he was going to continue.

Miss Vivee interjected. "Can we see the gardens?"

"Oh sure," he said. "Let me get a golf cart. I'll take you over to Mrs. Wagner. She's over at the greenhouses right now." He checked his watch. "She'll give you the red carpet tour."

"Can't we drive over?" Miss Vivee asked. "Logan always drives me around, and I feel most comfortable in her Jeep."

Where did that come from? She hates my jeep.

"Oh sure," he said. "I just wanted to help." He scratched his arm, and ran his hand over his hair. "Here, let me help you get back in the car and I can give you some directions. It's real easy to get where she is."

"Okay. Thanks," I said and walked over to the driver's side to get in.

"It's really something to see you here, Mrs. Pennywell. After yesterday," he said closing her car door. "But as my grandmother always told me, it's a small world. What a coincidence, huh?"

"You quote your grandmother?" Miss Vivee asked. "How nice."

"She was smart," Gavin said. "She knew something about everything. She raised me after my mother died."

"Where was your father?" Miss Vivee asked.

She's so nosey.

Gavin hunched his shoulders. "He wasn't around. Left right after I was born. Broke my mother's heart."

"Aw, well a grandmother's all one really needs anyway," Miss Vivee said. "My grandson wouldn't trade me for a mother or a father."

I shook my head. "So why were you over at the fairgrounds yesterday?" I said. I couldn't remember if he'd told us or not.

"I don't think you've told me your name," he said in a voice much different than the one he used with Miss Vivee. He even seemed to glare at me, I wasn't sure because Miss Vivee got his attention and he let his eyes go to her.

"That's Logan," she said.

"I told you, *Logan*," he said emphasizing my name. "It was part of my job."

"How was it part of your job?" Miss Vivee asked.

I did want to know that, but I wasn't asking any more questions.

"Because," he said to her, his tone returning back to a friendlier cadence. "Mr. Wagner owns Lincoln Park. He owns – well *owned* – all that land. They were short-handed so I was assigned to work over there for the day."

"I say," Miss Vivee said.

"Yep," Gavin nodded. "His family has had that lot for years. They're the ones that planted all the flowers there."

"I thought Mrs. Wagner was the flower person," Miss Vivee said.

"She is," Gavin said. "She knows a lot, you'll see. And her prize possession is the Poison Garden."

Chapter Eleven

She was in her late fifties, her brown hair mostly hidden by a wide-brimmed, rolled straw hat. She was perched on a small three-legged stool, her turquoise garden gloved hands were deep in the dirt. A flat of flowers sat next to her.

We had taken a winding back road around the perimeter of the gardens, and had parked in a small parking area to the side of a series of various sized greenhouses.

Camren Wagner was in front of one of the larger structures. She was so absorbed in her work she hadn't heard us walk up.

"I think that the outside of a greenhouse should be just as floral as the inside," Miss Vivee said.

The woman tending to the flowers turned, startled to see us. "This is a private area," she said with a distinct Southern twang. "No one's allowed back here."

"Hello," Miss Vivee said. "We're looking for the owners of the property. Is Mrs. Krieger around?"

Miss Vivee knew that woman's name was not Krieger.

Mrs. Wagner dug her trowel into the ground and stood up. She glanced down at her gloved hands and slapped them one against the other, back and forth a few times shaking off the dirt. Then she pulled them off and dropped them on the ground next to her flowers.

"I'm Camren Wagner." She walked over to us at the end of the sidewalk. "I own the property. But as you can see, I'm busy right now." She spoke slowly, drawing her words out so that it accentuated her accent. "And I don't see visitors back here." She pulled a walkie-talkie phone from a clip on the waistband of her shorts, apparently ready to get help to remove us.

"Oooo!" Miss Vivee clutched her chest. I froze, ready for anything because I wouldn't put it past her to fake a heart attack or something. "Isn't that a Middlemist Red?" Miss Vivee pointed to a bright pink flower that resembled, at least to me, a rose. She walked down the sidewalk outside the greenhouse to get a better look. I followed her just in case her sudden chest pang was real. "That is probably the rarest flowering plant in the world."

"No," Camren Wagner shook her head. She watched Miss Vivee from the other end of the walkway. "It's not a Middlemist Red."

"It is," Miss Vivee said with a sly grin crawling up her face. "You can't fool me, and for it to be doing so well," she pointed at the flower. "You must be very good at what you do. To be able to cultivate it here." Miss Vivee batted her eyes, and it seemed like she'd developed a Southern accent of her own. "Have you ties to Britain?"

What did that have to do with anything? I wondered.

"No," Camren seemed to blush.

Then Miss Vivee pointed to the flat of flowers that Camren had had next to her when we walked up. "Land sakes alive! Are those chocolate Cosmos?" She glanced at Mrs. Wagner. "They survive only as anon fertile clones." Miss Vivee shook her head and walked over to the rich deep red flowers. I would've thought they were pansies.

"Yes, they are," Camren nodded her head.

Shows what I know.

"You, my dear are a miracle worker. I can smell the vanillin from here." Miss Vivee bent down and inhaled. "How did you get them?" Miss Vivee asked.

Camren shook her head like she wasn't quite sure what to say.

"Well, I could tell you how I got mine," Miss Vivee said. "But then my husband would have to come and bail me out of jail. Again." They both laughed and Camren clipped her walkie-talkie back on her hip.

"Hey!" A man came around the corner, a big smile on his face, apparently not seeing us so far down the walkway. "I've been calling-" He stopped mid-sentence. "Sorry," he said after rounding the corner and noticing us standing there. "I didn't know anyone else would be here."

"That's because no one is allowed back here," Miss Vivee said and look at him warily.

As if she wasn't trespassing.

He certainly didn't appear to work at the gardens. He wore a very expensive-looking suit, shiny brown leather loafers, and dangled a Mercedes key chain. He was fair-skinned, had an angular jaw line, goldilocks lips – not full, not thin and a cupid's bow not rounded, not peaked – and freckles that covered practically every inch of his face.

"Maybe we could follow you back out?" Miss Vivee said. I knew she was trying to get a reaction out of him.

"No," Camren said, obviously she'd rather not dispense with us than to have to explain why that man was there. She looked at Miss Vivee. "It's alright. What is it that you need?"

"I'm Vivienne Caspard-Whitson," she said.

Caspard? Where did she get that name from?

"And this is my caregiver, Logan." I nodded my head and stepped back, capitulating to the low status she'd just given me.

"And you're Mr. Wagner?" Miss Vivee walked up to the well-dressed man and held out a limp hand. "Pleasure to meet you," she said.

The man took her hand, and coughed out a "No."

"No. No." Camren Wagner said, speaking up. "This is a, uhm, business associate." She glanced at him and back at us. "Robert Bernard." He gave his acknowledgement with a nod. "Bobby, say 'Hello,'" Mrs. Wagner directed.

With a hint of genuflection, hands stuffed in his pockets, Robert Bernard mumbled a "Hello." to us.

"So you were saying?" Camren Wagner turned back to Miss Vivee

"Oh yes." Miss Vivee shook her head as if trying to clear her thoughts. "My husband and I are looking to leave our land to someone when we die," Miss Vivee said glossing over him after the introduction. "We never had children and we've seemed to have outlived everyone we cared about." She hung her head appearing sad. "I heard about how people leave their land for arboretums and gardens and thought that would be a good use for our land. We'd rather give it to private owners than let the state take it over after we're gone."

"Are you two gardeners?" Camren Wagner asked. "You and your husband?"

"Oh, yes." Miss Vivee smiled a smile that made her whole face glow. "Did you think I was just a purloiner of rare and exotic flowers?"

"Oh no!" Camren put her hand to her face as if she was embarrassed.

"I have a greenhouse, too. Nothing as extravagant," Miss Vivee spread out her arm, "but very expansive."

"Where is your land located?" Robert Bernard seemed to take an interest in Miss Vivee's big lie.

"Are you a gardener?" Miss Vivee asked him.

Didn't know how she'd answer his question about her land, probably why she side-stepped it. The only land she owned was the plot that the Maypop sat atop of.

"No," he said, and noticed Miss Vivee's instant frown. "But I'm a land developer," he continued. "I have investments all over Georgia."

"Do say?" Miss Vivee tilted her head. "And what exactly does a land developer do?"

It was easy to see that Robert Bernard was proud of what he did. He stood up straighter, took his hand out of his pockets, and gave what seemed like a well-rehearsed, almost textbook narration of his work. "I procure land and decide the best use for it – how to develop it appropriately," he said. "And then I ensure the land is developed not only to how I see fit, but so it's in compliance with zoning ordinances – local, federal laws and what not. And I am usually the one to oversee every inch of the construction of it, be it residential, commercial or industrial structures."

"You do all of that on your own?"

"Well, no. But I do have my own business." He cleared his throat. "And I work with other companies."

"And how can you be sure what the best use of a land is?" Miss Vivee asked tilting her head the other way.

"Well," he gesticulated with his hands. "I make projections that assess potential profitability."

"That sounds hard," Miss Vivee said. "Deciding what to build where."

"It can be difficult. But if you know what you're doing," he said, "it isn't as hard as it may sound. It's based on research proposition. I conduct studies on population growth, traffic patterns, local taxes then I know what's best."

"That's a lot of big words, Mr. Bernard," Miss Vivee said. She looked at Camren Wagner. "We're just simple folk. We've got a few thousand acres of land left to my grandfather in a land grant for his service in the military during the Civil War. Maybe you've heard of him, Capt. Albert Caspard?"

Oh that's where the name Caspard came from. I wonder if he was even a real person.

I was tempted to pull out my phone and Google him.

"A couple of thousand?" Robert Bernard swallowed hard and swiped a hand through his gelled auburn hair.

"We were out for a drive, and saw your beautiful land." Miss Vivee kept up with her con and ignored Robert Bernard. "It is much more than I could have ever imagine for our land. Your place is truly wonderful. Delightful," she said nodding her head.

"Thank you," Camren Wagner said, her face flushed and a gleam in her eye.

Boy was Miss Vivee winning her over.

"That's why." Miss Vivee cozied up to Camren Wagner as if she were her new best friend. "We'd rather chose you and your husband over an implacable land baron."

Miss Vivee flashed a big ole smile, and I could tell by Robert Bernard's face – pleased then confused – that he wasn't sure if Miss Vivee's remark was meant as a jeer at him or not.

"That's very generous of you, Mrs. Whitson," Camren Wagner said.

"It's *Caspard*-Whitson, but you can call me Vivienne."

"You never did say where that land was located," Robert Bernard said.

"In the Black Belt." Miss Vivee raised an eyebrow. "That's why we've got to be careful what's done with it." Miss Vivee cut her eyes at Mr. Bernard. Her glare made his face redden so much that all of his freckles seemed to merge.

And what is the Black Belt? I wondered. Probably more of her lies.

Miss Vivee looked over at me. "You know, Logan, I think I want Mr. and Mrs. Wagner to have our land." She put her hand on Camren's arm. "I think that the two of us are kindred spirits."

"Like I said, Vivienne, that is very generous of you." Camren Wagner smiled genuinely at her. "I don't know if we . . . If I could. You see there is no Mr. Wagner. Not anymore."

"Oh no!" Miss Vivee feigned surprise. "Are you divorced?"

"No," she said. "Widowed. Just yesterday."

"Was it a heart attack?" Miss Vivee asked innocently.

"Why yes. Yes it was," Widow Wagner confirmed the story she'd told at the fair.

"Oh honey," Miss Vivee said, acting as if she was all choked up. I could have sworn I even saw her eyes get misty. "No wonder you're out here with all of these beauties. They take away all the pain, don't they?"

"Yes, they do," she said and hung her head.

Geesh. No one would have guessed she had any pain when her husband was splayed out in the Judges Tent and she was playing Bob Barker.

"Why don't you show me around?" Miss Vivee said. "I'd love a tour. And I know that'll cheer you up."

"I did need to speak to you, Camren," Robert Bernard said.

"Well, she's busy now," Miss Vivee said rudely. "And it really isn't polite to talk business right after a death in the family." Miss Vivee cocked her head to the side. "You weren't raised in the South, were you?"

"Can it wait, Bobby?" Camren asked. "I'll give you call this afternoon. Is that alright?"

"Bobby" squinted his eyes and blew out a huff. "I guess it'll have to be alright." He turned to Miss Vivee as if he wanted to say something, but instead turned on his heels and marched back out toward the parking lot.

"I don't think you should do business with him," Miss Vivee said. "He seems like such a grouch."

Camren laughed.

I can't wait to see your gardens," Miss Vivee said.

"Well then, let me go and get a golf cart so I can show them to you. Might be too much for you to walk."

"That'll be fine," she said. "But I'm an avid golfer you know, so I'm used to walking the fairways. They didn't have golf carts until the late 1950s, and after walking around all those years, I saw no need to hop into one."

"You don't look old enough to have played golf in the '50s," Camren said.

Oh goodness, now she's taken to lying, too.

Miss Vivee giggled. "You get the cart. Is there enough room for Logan?"

"Oh yes," she glanced over at me. "I can't wait to show you around," Camren said.

"Good," Miss Vivee said. "I can't wait to see everything. And I've heard you have a poison garden?"

"Yes, we do. Our prized possession," Camren said and smile.

"Good," Miss Vivee said. "I want to see that first.

Chapter Twelve

And the Poison Garden was the first place we went. It was set apart from the rest of the gardens, near the back, it was enclosed within an antique-looking, ornate, black wrought iron fence. The Widow Wagner walked us under the high archway that depicted birds and cherubs, and into what I would imagine the Secret Garden looked like. There was a paved walkway that encircled the area and flowers everywhere in between.

I didn't know there were so many kinds of poisonous flowers.

"You have a nice collection," Miss Vivee said. "Your display choices are good." She smiled at Camren then looked at me and shook her head. "But you have a lot missing," Miss Vivee said to her.

"I do?" she said. "It's certainly not meant to be complete, but I thought I had it pretty well covered. Still there's another piece of land we own. It's just an open field right now, but as it'll be all mine now-" she sucked in a breath as if she realized she said something she shouldn't have. "I have plans on something more extensive."

"It's lovely here," Miss Vivee said and patted Camren on her arm. "You've done a wonderful job."

I didn't know what it was that Widow Wagner was worried spilling the beans about, but I took Miss Vivee's actions and words to mean that all the flowers that were on that note weren't there. But that didn't stop her from taking it all in. Miss Vivee and Camren Wagner walked through the garden, at one point, arm-in-arm, and chatted about the flowers. I followed behind, not saying much. I figured a caregiver shouldn't speak.

"What else do you have to show me?" Miss Vivee asked as we rounded back to the gate.

"You want to see more?" Camren asked. "You're not tired?"

"I may be old, but I'm fit," she said. "But Logan," she pointed a finger at me. "She doesn't get much exercise."

Why does she always put me in her lies?

"I'm fine," I said. "But you two enjoy yourselves." I figured that maybe, as part of her act, Miss Vivee wanted to be alone with Camren. I never could follow her methods, so it didn't bother me to stay behind. "Is there somewhere I can wait?"

"Let me show you," Camren said and looked at Miss Vivee. "I know you said you can walk, Mrs. Caspard-"

"Vivienne. Remember? Call me Vivienne."

"Okay," Camren said and smiled. "Vivienne. I know you said you could walk, but I'm just going to drive us up to the center of the gardens. Logan can wait for us there, and then we can walk. Is that okay?"

"Yes. That's fine," Miss Vivee said.

"Good. We don't usually bring the cart onto the grounds, but I'd feel better about you not having to walk that far."

We hopped on the golf cart and drove to the main gardens. We entered the garden area, and like the entrance there was a center fountain. This one much larger, though. From the middle of the fountain stood a greenish figure of a naked man carved out of a smooth stone. He had one hand stretched toward the sky, the other folded at his waist. He looked upward and water sprouted all around him. The fountain had a marble base with a border around the top wide enough for sitting. Water bubbled up from the bottom of it as well, shooting almost as high as the center figure at what seemed like timed intervals. Just the sound of the water was soothing.

But then, along the four walkways that branched out from the fountain, there was a profusion of flowers. Each section had a little sign that pointed the way to different gardens with a bench next to it. I couldn't see how there could be more flowers than the ones right in front of us.

The sun was rising in the sky, and its light seemed to make the flowers glimmer. There were butterflies and a sweet fragrance that filled the air. Miss Vivee almost jumped up with glee when she saw all the flowers. She nearly hopped off the cart and acted like a kid in a toy store - which one to see first.

Camren Wagner noticed her excitement. "Here," she said. "Let me show you what we have."

We got off the golf cart and circled the perimeter of the fountain. Camren spouted out flower names, the varieties and their origins like she was reciting the alphabet.

"And down each pathway are more flowers?" Miss Vivee asked noticing the signs. Her face was beaming.

"Yes," Camren Wagner said nodding and smiling.

"Well let's see them!" She said to Camren then turned to me. "You stay here," she ordered.

"You can wait here, by the fountain," Camren said in a nicer tone than the one Miss Vivee had used. Then she turned to Miss Vivee. "Are you ready? We can't stay too long, I have work, but there is a lot I can show you."

"Wait," Miss Vivee said to Camren Wagner, then looked at me. "Help me." She walked over to me. "Hold this." She handed me her purse, clicked the clasp open, and then dug down in it. "I need to put my sunglasses on." She pulled out her prescription glasses, then as per her usual, put her sunglasses on top.

Camren Wagner chuckled. "They make prescription sunglasses, you know?" She looked at me. "You should know that if you're her caregiver."

Yeah, I do know that, I thought. *And I've told her that a thousand times.*

"They make them all in one?" Miss Vivee asked as if it was the first she'd heard of it. "Why haven't you suggested that to me," she said, looking at me and tilting her head. "I would really like something like that. Wearing two pair can be so cumbersome."

"Yes," Mrs. Wagner said. "Perhaps you should think of getting some better help." Her accent much stronger, she looked at me down her nose and took Miss Vivee's arm. They started to stroll down one of the pathways, but were still in earshot.

"I know," I heard Miss Vivee say. "But I just feel bad for her, bless her heart. Sometimes she needs more help than I do, if you know what I mean?"

I plopped down on a bench and watched as they disappeared down a path. I didn't know if all of that was part of her act or not, but then and there I decided I would get Miss Vivee a pair of corrective lens sunglasses. I'd find out from Renmar her optometrist and get a copy of the prescription. I remembered my mother had gotten my grandfather a pair from Walmart.

Whether she really wanted them or not.

I took in a breath, blew it out and checked the clock on my phone.

Wonder how long they'll be gone . . .

I took a look around and smiled. What could be a better place than this to wait? I stood up and walked around the fountain and took in the beauty of the flowers that Jack's widow had shown us with pride. There were hundreds of them. Flowers of all colors and sizes, and from places all over the world. She had pointed to each and named it – snap dragons, dahlia, Gerber daisies, geraniums, petunia, and gladiolas, I remembered her rattling them off.

Yep, I thought and surveyed the flowers at my feet, *I remember the names, but I know I can't point out which is which.*

Camren Wagner knew her stuff.

Oh, I chuckled, *except for that sweet potato vine. I'll always remember that one.*

I leaned in and touched one of the wide leaves. The vine-like chartreuse and purple foliage of the plant had stuck with me because it didn't look anything like the top of a potato.

Miss Vivee was right, they were stirring and inspiring.

Then that note popped into my head.

I thought about that poem and how it had listed all those poisonous flowers. I had looked at it again while Miss Vivee bathed and washed her hair after we had decided to come to Krieger's Garden. I had sat down on her bed and tried to memorize it. My mother had an eidetic memory and I had wished for one as I read. But I did it.

I went over it, and over it again until I had seared that poem into my brain. That note seemed to bother Miss Vivee so much. I wanted to know it – to learn it, understand it, and maybe – hopefully – solve it.

I knew though that even if Miss Vivee didn't remember the entire poem, she remembered the name of each and every flower on it. And I wasn't sure, but I think she'd signaled to me that she hadn't seen all of them. Maybe that was why she wanted to look at more flowers.

I walked over to the fountain and sat down. Staring into the blue-green water, one line of the poem came to mind.

"So harken, and I will tell you true, for this will be your only clue . . ."

What was the clue?

I ran my hand through the water and thought about the poem. The flowers were listed after that line. Were the flowers the clue? Or did it just mean that the flowers were deadly? Something that just everyone wouldn't know. I hadn't known that fact until Miss Vivee told me.

Or was it a clue to the murder – or murderer?

I got up and flung the water off my hand, and rubbed it dry on my jeans. I walked over to a section of flowers, and standing among them I wanted to do just what the poem had told me to do.

Hidden within, the truth they belie. Listen closely, and you can hear . . .

I sat down on the bench. "Listen closely," I whispered and bent over the arm of the bench to get closer to a row of white flowers. "What truth do you belie?"

"What in the world are you doing?" Miss Vivee said and startled me. I sat up straight. "You act as if you've never smelled a flower before."

Chapter Thirteen

"Did they have all the flowers that were in the note," I asked Miss Vivee as we pulled out the parking lot from Krieger Arboretum's greenhouses.

"No," Miss Vivee said and nothing more.

Okay, I thought. *Maybe she doesn't want to talk about it.*

I prayed Camren Wagner didn't talk to Gavin Tanner before we could leave the grounds because with his talkative self I knew he would have blown our cover. I could just picture her on her walkie-talkie summoning guards who'd block us in. But we got back to the entrance and through the archway of trees without a hitch.

I took the exit for the highway and glanced over at Miss Vivee. She took off her glasses, put them away, and stared out of the window. She had a look on her face that told me she was lost in thought. I didn't want to disturb her. I knew that that note, with all the flowers she had in her garden, was on her mind.

I need to help her find a place that has all those flowers.

I decided to go back to the fairgrounds. Miss Vivee needed to see the flowers there again. Maybe there were new flowers there. Some that hadn't been there when that sixty-five-year-old murder happened. New ones. Ones she hadn't noticed when we were there, perhaps they were planted in an area other than where we had been. Lincoln Park was big. It couldn't hurt, I reasoned, to swing by there and let her get a closer look. Might even make her feel better.

Without telling her, I took the exit ramp off of I-520 that led to the state route and Lincoln Park.

"Where are you taking me?" Miss Vivee asked.

"I have an errand to run," I lied. She did it all the time so I figured my one tiny lie wasn't such a bad thing.

The flowers were visible from a half a mile down the road from the entrance to the fairgrounds. There was a whole field of them. And as soon as I saw them, it popped into my head that it was odd just to have a field with flowers. A waste of land use (using Robert Bernard's words), and money wasted on landscaping on a backroad field that many people didn't see. Did they do anything else on the land other than have the fair once a year?

"Is this your errand?" Miss Vivee asked interrupting my thoughts as I pulled up in the parking lot. "Coming to the fairgrounds?"

But before I could answer her, or get Miss Vivee to pay attention to the flowers, she noticed an old Volkswagen van covered in them. They were painted in psychedelic colors, and interspersed with peace and love symbols and words.

"Will you looka there?" Miss Vivee pointed to the Volkswagen in the parking lot. "That's Martha Simmons' van."

"Oh crap," I said. "The killer pie lady?" I asked. "Please don't tell me you know her."

"Don't say that." Miss Vivee swatted her hand across my arm. "Her pie didn't kill that man. They haven't always been the tastiest things, but lately her pies are much better. Amazingly better."

"She told me that her pies had always won every contest she entered them in."

"Well, I don't know about that, but they have always won first place at the Freemont County Possum Pickin' Fair." Miss Vivee bit her bottom lip. "But I do know that they never killed anyone. Not even when they were bad."

"I'm not so sure," I said. "They certainly made everyone sick."

"Well, when we see her, don't you say anything about that."

We got out of my jeep and walked into the fairgrounds. Miss Vivee yanked open the flap to the Plethora of Pie tent and like the last time I'd seen it, it was dark and deserted.

"Maybe no one's here," I offered.

"Nonsense, I'd know that Peace Mobile anywhere. That's Martha's van. Rode in it plenty of times."

What was this thing, people keeping vehicles twenty and thirty years? With all the snow and salted roads in Cleveland, I was used to people changing cars every three or four years.

"Yoohoo!" Miss Vivee called out. "Martha? You here? I dropped by to give my congratulations." She walked around the cherry pie counter and toward the back leaving me near the entrance. "Yoohoo, Martha!"

Aunt Martha peeked out from the curtained prep area. "Vivienne!" she nearly shouted and came out with her arms outstretched. "So nice to see a familiar face," she said and hugged Miss Vivee. Tightly.

Miss Martha still donned her salmon color apron, but this time she wore a brown, cotton shift dress underneath. Her brown hair perfectly coiffed.

"I say." Miss Vivee held her head up, and outside of the hug, she stretched one hand up to give Aunt Martha a limp pat on the back. She acted as if she couldn't breathe in Aunt Martha's unyielding embrace.

"What are you doing still here?" Miss Vivee asked, having to put a little *ump* into wrenching from Aunt Martha's grip.

"I had orders from people at the fair, and I told them to pick them up here because I still had to come and get my equipment." Aunt Martha sniffed as she spoke, and after she let go of Miss Vivee it as obvious her eyes, like her cheeks and nose, were a rosy red.

"What in the Sam Hill is wrong with you?" Miss Vivee asked noticing her face.

Marigold came out from the back, just as Aunt Martha was dabbing her nose, and getting ready to tell Miss Vivee what she was crying about. Marigold had on blue jeans and a faded gray T-shirt with Stanford written in red across the front.

My alma mater.

"What's wrong, Nana?" Marigold asked.

"Nana?" Miss Vivee said and smiled. "Is this your granddaughter, Martha?"

"Yes," Aunt Martha said, her face brightening up. "This is my granddaughter, Marigold. Marigold Kent." She pulled Marigold close to her. "Isn't she beautiful?" Aunt Martha asked.

"Yes, she is," Miss Vivee said.

"And although she'd never admit it, she's a first-rate baker."

"Really?" Miss Vivee said.

Marigold spoke up. "Not really," she said and chuckled. "My grandmother says it's in my blood, I should just be a natural at it, but I burn everything I put my hands on."

"Nonsense," Aunt Martha said. "Now, Marigold, this is Vivienne Pennywell, an old and dear friend," finishing up her introduction. "And this is -" She turned to me and stopped mid-sentence. Taking a good look at me for the first time, she hissed, "Good Lord! "What are you doing here?"

Miss Vivee turned to me and back to Martha. "What is it?"

"What is she doing here?" Aunt Martha asked. "She's the one that accused my pie of making people sick."

"Oh *pfft*! She didn't mean no harm." Miss Vivee beckoned me. "This is Bay's girl." She nodded in a knowing way and leaned into Aunt Martha. "She's from up north, bless her heart."

"Oh," Aunt Martha said as if that explained everything.

I felt foolish just standing around while they discussed me. But Marigold, seemingly not remembering her disdain for me just the day before, smiled at me and nodded a hello.

"Okay, well," Aunt Martha started, "Where's your manners, Vivienne? Introduce her."

"This is Logan Dickerson. She's an archaeologist and soon to be granddaughter."

At least I'd moved up the career ladder with this introduction.

"Really?" Aunt Martha said. She and Marigold looked at me. "There was a doctor at the fair that said she was *his* granddaughter."

"Oh. That was probably Mac," Miss Vivee said and turned to me. I nodded. "You remember Mac, Martha. Macomber Whitson?"

"Oh! From way back when?" Aunt Martha asked her memory apparently jarred. "That Mac?"

"Yes," Miss Vivee said. "*That* Mac."

"Well, I must admit I was kind of dumbfounded, but Marigold set me straight. She fussed that today there are blended families and I shouldn't make a big deal with her being . . . well you know, not the same as he was," she shot Marigold a smile. "You know, she uses the computer to study that ancestry stuff-"

"Genealogy," Marigold corrected.

"Whatever," Aunt Martha flapped a hand toward Marigold. "Had me racking my brains to remember our family's history. Signing stuff, even swabbing my mouth for some mail in DDA test."

"DNA, Nana."

"Right," Aunt Martha said and smiled at Marigold. "But now I understand." She nodded at me. "She's Bay's girl."

I looked at Miss Vivee. She didn't like people saying things about Bay, especially about him being half black. Bay had told me that his grandmother was the one who taught him to stand up to people who bullied him because he was the only black kid in the neighborhood. But Aunt Martha's remarks didn't seem to faze her.

We heard a horn honk and everyone turned around to see a man and a boy getting out of a car.

"Oh! That's my customer," Aunt Martha said. "I'll be right back."

She disappeared into the back, and Marigold called out to her. "I'll come help you, Nana," she said.

"No," Martha shouted from the back. "Keep our visitor company." Aunt Martha reappeared from behind the curtain with four pink boxes stacked high, nearly covering her face. "I've got this," she said sounding a little winded. She walked toward the front and met the man outside of the tent.

An uncomfortable silence hung in the air until Marigold spoke up.

"So you're an archaeologist?" Marigold asked. "Like Indiana Jones?"

"That would be my mother," I said. "I'm just the run-of-the-mill kind."

"I didn't know there was a run-of-the-mill one. I mean you don't run into one every day."

"No you don't," I said and smiled.

"So you kind of study genealogy too, huh?" Marigold asked me. "In a roundabout way."

I chuckled. "I guess I do. It's important to know family lineages when studying ancient civilizations and relating it to the people of today."

"Tell that to my grandmother. She doesn't seem to understand that at all. I tried to do a genealogy for her side of the family and she can't remember anything." She gave me a sly smile. "No help, I swear. But I have my ways of finding out what I need to know."

I laughed. With my degree in anthropology, and all of my experience in looking at the lives of other people, I'd never thought to do one of my own family.

"How do you become an archaeologist?" Marigold asked. "Is it like an apprentice program or is it a major? I've never heard anyone majoring in Archaeology."

"I actually got my graduate degree at Stanford." I pointed to her T-shirt. "And they do have an undergraduate degree in it."

"Really?" she raised her eyebrows. "I didn't know they offered archaeology there."

"Yep." I nodded in affirmation. "They do. I didn't go there for my bachelor's, though, I went to school in Ohio, where I'm from. And my graduate degree is in Anthropology with a track in archaeology."

"Oh," she said.

"What did you study at Stanford?"

"I have a degree in Nutrition."

I had a questioning look on my face that she must have noticed. She may not have known that they offered archaeology at Stanford, but I knew for a fact they didn't offer nutrition as a major.

I looked at her then down at her shirt. She followed my gaze and rubbed her palm down the front of it. "I didn't get my degree at Stanford. Not that smart," she said and smiled. "I participated in their annual Food Summit."

I nodded my head. "Food Summit."

"Did someone say food?" Miss Vivee said and looked around questioningly. "I'm hungry."

Marigold and I laughed at Miss Vivee's comment. "It's given by the Nutrition Studies Research Group," Marigold finished her explanation. "That's a part of the Stanford Prevention Research Center."

"Oh, I see," I said.

"Well, you have a degree in nutrition," Miss Vivee said. "You must can cook."

That brought another round of laughter from the two of us.

"Doesn't mean I can cook," Marigold said. "Nutrition is the study of food. I may study how it's done, but definitely can't do it myself."

"Where did you go?" I asked. "To get your degree?"

"University of California," she said. "I just stayed close to home, too."

"Home?" Miss Vivee said. She didn't seem to really be following our conversation, she just hopped in to comment when she heard something that piqued her interest.

"Yup." Marigold nodded.

"Didn't you grow up in Lincoln?"

"Where?" Marigold asked.

"Nebraska?" Miss Vivee said. "Lincoln, Nebraska?"

"No!" Marigold chuckled. "We are California girls," she said. "'West coast. The cutest girls in the world.' At least according to the Beach Boys, and my dad."

"Your Nana too?" Miss Vivee asked. "She lived in California?"

"Yes. Oh, but now that you mentioned it, she had a close friend that lived in Nebraska. I don't think it was Lincoln though. But I don't remember if she ever visited her, I just remember her talking about her."

"Do tell," Miss Vivee said and smiled.

Chapter Fourteen

"Where to, Miss Vivee?" I hopped in my side of the car after pushing her into the passenger seat. I reached over and buckled her seat belt.

"I hate this car," she said.

"Yes, Miss Vivee, I know."

"Why can't you have a sensible car? I don't understand why you have to sit up so high." She looked over at me. "Does it make you feel better than others? Being able to look down on them?"

"No," I shook my head and chuckled. "Lots of people have trucks. SUVs. They're very popular."

"Well, I wouldn't give a wooden nickel for one."

"Yeah, I've seen your style of vehicles," I said and glanced over at her. Miss Vivee owned a boat for a car, a 1994, gas guzzling, "Mow-Your-Man-Down, Lincoln Town Car." It was the reason that Mac walked with a limp.

"Let's go over Mac's house," she said. "We'll sit a spell, then we can go to Jellybean's and have lunch. Maybe Viola knows something about this Camren Wagner."

"Go to Mac's house?" I turned and stared at her. A surprise look on my face. "Do you mean like on the inside of it?"

"Yes. To his house," she said adjusting her seatbelt, like she didn't understand my surprise. "Inside. Sit down. Visit. Chew the fat." She glanced at me. "Please don't start acting weird again."

"I'm not acting weird. I'm just wondering about you and your vow."

"What in the world are you talking about? We've been to Mac's house plenty of times."

"We" hadn't ever been to Mac's house, let alone "plenty of times."

Miss Vivee, twenty years earlier, had thought that Mac cheated on her with a woman that lived near him. That "floosy," as Miss Vivee called her, would visit Mac and bring him food. So she had vowed after that that she would never go inside of Mac's house again. But as of late, she'd eased her way back in. First, she'd have me to take her to his house to pick him up, graduating to "sitting for a spell" on his front porch for a glass of iced tea, to finally going inside. Sure she'd spent time with him, but never with me. I only got to be the chauffeur.

"Does Mac know we're coming?" I asked.

"No."

"You want me to call first?" I said reaching for my phone.

"Why in the world would you need to call him?"

I put the car in drive and went to Mac's and didn't say another word about it.

Mac's house was large for just him and his dog. I'd known that from sitting outside of it when I come to pick him up. But it was even larger than I thought once I finally got to see the inside of it. I first bent over and ruffled up his dog, Rover, who greeted us with two large barks, and then took in the place

It was made like the Maypop. There was a large foyer that had a staircase in the middle of it, a long hallway that led to the back of the house, and several rooms to each side of the stairs. But where the Maypop was bright, shiny and scrubbed as clean as a Marine's boot, Mac's house was cluttered. Not dirty, just in a state of dishevel.

There were books and magazines everywhere. Mostly medical – AMA periodicals and textbooks – but also almanacs, National Geographics, and even a stack of tech magazines, which surprised me because he was always telling me to "gaggle" something instead of "Google" it.

All these books. No wonder he knew so much, all he did was read.

"May I have a glass of water," Miss Vivee asked. "I'm parched."+

"Sure" Mac said. "C'mon back."

He led us down the hallway into a cheery, country kitchen. There were black and white gingham curtains bordered with bright red cherries hung at the three windows. The floor was checkered black and white with a big, red woven rug in the middle of it. An old style 1950s kitchen table and chairs with red seat cushions sat on top of it, which he pointed to. "Have a seat," he directed us.

"You want ice, Vivee?" Mac asked and pulled a pitcher of water out of a refrigerator that looked as old as the table and chairs.

"No. If it's cold, I don't need any ice."

"It's ice cold," he said and pulled a glass out of the cabinet. "You want a glass, Logan."

"No thank you, Mac," I said.

He poured the water and started to take the container back to the refrigerator.

"Leave that pitcher out," she said. "I'm sure I'll drink the whole thing."

Mac sat down at the table with us and placed the pitcher in front of Miss Vivee. "So did you find someplace else that had all the flowers?" Mac asked.

"No," I said.

"Yes," Miss Vivee said and took a big gulp of water.

"No," I said again.

Miss Vivee dismissed my answer with a wave of her hand and put her glass on the table. "We went to an arboretum up near Augusta. They had a Poison Garden there."

"What is that?" he asked.

"A garden that showcases beautiful, deadly flowers," she said.

"Isn't that what your note said?" Mac asked.

"It's not my note, Mac. It's the killer's note. But, yes, that's what it said," Miss Vivee said. "And I'm sure that woman at the arboretum had something to do with Jack Wagner's death."

"What woman, Vivee?" Mac asked.

"Camren Wagner."

"I thought you liked her," I said and scrunched up my nose. "Why are you calling her 'that woman?'"

"Whatever gave you the idea I liked her?" Miss Vivee frowned at me.

"You," I said. "I got that idea from you. You and Mrs. Wagner seemed to get along famously."

"We did not," Miss Vivee said. "That show-off walked around, with her chest stuck out, talking with that phony accent, trying to make herself into something she wasn't. Planting rare flowers *outside* of the greenhouse, *hmf*!"

"Her accent wasn't phony," I said.

"Phony as a two-dollar bill."

"Vivee, you know that now they make two dollar bills." Mac said.

"They do?" she asked. "No, I didn't know. No one told me that." She looked at me. "Then phony as a three-dollar bill." She turned to Mac. "They don't make those do they, Mac?"

"No, Sweetie."

"Good," Miss Vivee said and turned back to me. "I only made nice to her to get some information."

"So, now who is this Camren Wagner?" Mac asked. "Jack's wife?"

"Yes. They own that place."

Mac chuckled. "Don't that just beat all? So you think she's the one who did it? Killed her husband with a botanical poison?"

"Jury's still out on that one. Couple of things bothering me about the whole thing," Miss Vivee said. "But she does has every flower on that note."

"Does she now?" Mac said.

"No," I said again, but neither one of them seem to notice me.

"I couldn't wait to get here to tell you," Miss Vivee said, the gleam in her eye disappearing as she looked at me. "But Miss Ann over here," she pointed at me," backtracked, taking me all over Augusta County. That's why I'm so thirsty." She took a sip of her water. "Been riding around in that jeep of hers in the hot sun all morning."

Miss Ann? That's a new name for me.

"What's going on?" Mac asked. "What'dya find out?"

"It's a big breakthrough in the case," she said seemingly tried to build up a little suspense in her relaying of the events.

"Breakthrough?" I made sure I was heard when I repeated her analysis of our visit to Krieger's Garden.

"Yes."

"Breakthrough in what, Miss Vivee? Because she didn't have all the flowers in her Garden. At least that's what you told me."

I went back over our walk through the gardens in my mind, and our conversation with everyone we'd seen, and I couldn't for the life of me think of anything we'd learned.

"Breakthrough on the murderer," she said as if she were disgusted with me.

"You found out something?" I asked in disbelief.

"Yes." Again a one word answer.

I was puzzled. I turned to Mac. "All of the flowers weren't there," I said. "She had some, I'm guessing and I don't know why Miss Vivee's telling you that she had them all because she didn't. She told me they didn't. That's why I took her back to the fairgrounds. To see if they had them there."

"Yes," she said to me. "She does have them all."

"No she doesn't, Miss Vivee." I shook my head. "I remember specifically you telling me she didn't have them all."

"I told you that she had all of them but one out there."

"Okay," I said. "You never told me that."

"Well I meant to tell you that."

Why do I even try to argue with her?

"Okay," I said trying to soften my voice. "She had them all but one. So that means you're still the only one with *all* of the flowers, and it doesn't help you with the note."

She turned to Mac. "Every one of those flowers mentioned on that note was there except for the lily."

"The Lily of the Valley?" Mac asked.

"Right," Miss Vivee said. "But, and here's the *breakthrough*," she emphasized that for my benefit I guessed. "They own the land where the fairgrounds are located."

"Ahhh," Mac said. "So she could have written that note. She has all the flowers."

"Yes," Miss Vivee said and nodded triumphantly.

"How?" I said. "How does she have all the flowers?" The two of them sometimes only used one brain to figure out stuff and I definitely wasn't privy to it.

"There are lilies all over that field," Mac told me. "In Lincoln Park. True lilies and flowering plants that look like lilies."

"Look like lilies?" I asked.

"Yes, like calla lily, fire lily, water lily, day lily," Mac explained. "They're not considered true lilies, but," he looked at Miss Vivee, "that field outside where they set up for the fair is full of them. Including the lily-of-the-valley."

I thought about it. *Maybe I did see a lily*.

I need to take a mini-botany class if I'm going to hang out with these two. I decided instead to Google them later.

"So, me taking you to the fairgrounds did help," I said and smiled. I'd pat myself on the back if she wouldn't.

"One way or another, she has every one of them," Miss Vivee said affirming her earlier comment. "And,

Abby L. Vandiver

she's a gardener. Had the most beautiful gardens I'd ever seen." Miss Vivee smiled at the memory.

"Did she?" Mac asked.

"But that's not the point," she got back on track. "Her having those flowers means she has the knowledge necessary to put that note together. She knew they were poisonous."

"That's true," Mac said. "But what's the reason for doing it?"

"That's the other thing I learned," Miss Vivee said. "Jack Wagner was all set to divorce her and leave her penniless."

"That's just gossip," I said and shook my head. "And no one said anything about her being penniless."

"Well that's certainly a motive," Mac said seemingly again not hearing what I'd said.

"And I think that that Mrs. Wagner may have even had an accomplice," Miss Vivee continued.

"Really now? And who would that've been?" Mac was hanging on Miss Vivee's every word.

"A paramour."

"Ahh," Mac said. "Her and her lover all set to live out their lives together on Mr. Wagner's money."

"Not too sure she's going to keep him around, though."

"The plot thickens," Mac said and clapped his hands together, then rubbed them back and forth.

"Oh brother," I said. "You two are making a mountain out of a molehill."

126

A thirty minute visit to the arboretum, and Miss Vivee's had the whole thing figured out. Other than telling them my name, she hadn't said one truthful thing to those people, why would she think the information they gave her was anything but?

"Miss Vivee," I said. "They could have just gotten a divorce. If she didn't want him anymore because she wanted someone else, or if he wanted to be free of her. That would have been the logical thing to do, not commit murder."

"That's what people think when they're not in the situation. But when you're involved in a bad marriage, murder tends to cross your mind. Often."

"Miss Vivee," I said. "I can't believe that."

"You'll see, Missy, being married ain't easy."

"I'd be a good husband, Vivee," Mac said. "I'd never cheat."

"You're too old to be anything but a good husband, Mac," Miss Vivee said.

"So then are you gonna marry me, Vivee? Make me an honest man?"

Honest man? What was he talking about? Had he been climbing into her window at night?

"When pigs fly," Miss Vivee said. "You couldn't handle what I've got to offer," she said. "Might kill ya."

"I wouldn't mind dying, just to get a chance."

"Oh my goodness!" I said and covered my ears. "Do I have to listen to this?"

"He started it," Miss Vivee said. "He's just like every other man." She shook her head. "A one track mind."

Mac grinned.

"Really, Miss Vivee," I said.

"C'mon, Mac," Miss Vivee stood up. "I'll let you buy my lunch," she said. "Seeing you have a need to feel more honorable." She grabbed her purse and headed toward the door.

Mac looked at me and winked. "I think I'm wearing her down." He grabbed his hat and cane and followed behind her out the door.

Chapter Fifteen

Every time I walked into the Jellybean Café, I felt like I had stepped into Munchkinland.

We had stopped at Hadley's Drug store to get Miss Vivee her suspect notebook and three No. 2 pencils. She wondered around the store, Mac in tow, examining everything, fussing about the price, and not looking to buy anything. We were met with the lunch crowd by the time we got to Jellybean's.

"Well if it ain't the three amigos," Glenda, the good witch, aka Viola Rose said as she greeted us.

"Hi," Mac and I said. Miss Vivee just gave a nod.

Tilting her head to the side, and one hand on her hip, Viola Rose directed her question to Miss Vivee. "And how y'all doing today?"

"I'm worn out," Miss Vivee said. "Logan drug me all over three counties this morning." She fanned her face with her hand. "And I'm so hungry I done gone white-eyed."

Viola Rose looked at me and smiled. "Do tell," she said. "Well let me get you seated, and see if I can't find a tall glass of sweet tea for you."

Viola Rose walked ahead of us, grabbing three menus she led us to a booth in the back. She was always sparkly, outspoken, and the town gossip, which was why Miss Vivee liked to come and see her (besides for the egg salad).

Today, Viola Rose had traded her usual pink sparkle and bedazzle for purple. Her wrist full of bangles clanked as she swatted a stray strand of her strawberry blonde hair that she kept swept up in a bouffant style out of her eyes. A black apron with deep pockets covered tight, metallic purple leggings, and a purple puckered shirt. She had on white running shoes, although I had never even seen her walk fast.

I waved to her munchkin-sized husband, Gus, who manned the kitchen. He was the opposite of Viola Rose, a permanent scowl on his face, he worked the kitchen in a white apron, t-shirt, chef's skull cap and the precision of a French-trained chef. He made a mean bacon cheeseburger, but with the crowd that came through the doors from six am to seven pm when they closed, I soon learned his skills weren't limited to All American food fare.

I slid into one side of the purple, orange and red striped benches, and Miss Vivee and Mac sat across from me. Viola Rose laid the menus in front of each of us.

"I'ma go get your sweet tea, Miss Vivee," Viola Rose said. "Everybody else want their usual?" she asked.

Mac and I nodded, and Viola Rose left to get our drinks.

"I didn't drag you through three counties, Miss Vivee," I said picking up the menu.

"I know," Miss Vivee said and waved her hand. "I just wanted Viola Rose to hurry and get us to our seats. She would have stood there for an hour and talked."

"Well I don't want you to have her thinking I'd let you starve just so I could drive around."

"Oh, that reminds me," Miss Vivee said to Mac. "Logan took me to the doctor's office this morning."

"Doctor's? Why? Is something wrong?" Mac asked concern on his face. "Why didn't you just come to see me?"

"We went to that elderly doctor that Renmar wants me to go to."

"A geriatrician?" Mac asked. "Why does she want you to do that?"

"Because she thinks I'm bonkers."

Viola Rose came just then and put down our drinks – sweet tea for Miss Vivee, a coke for me and coffee for Mac. She pulled three straws from her apron pocket. "I'll be right back to get your orders," she said.

"She does not think you're bonkers," I said after Viola Rose left. I turned to Mac. "She was just worried about Miss Vivee because she seemed out of sorts this morning."

"You'd be outta sorts, too, if you thought someone might accuse you of murder," Miss Vivee said and nodded her head. "At least I don't go around crying for no reason like that Martha Simmons."

I chuckled. "Yeah, what was wrong with her?"

"I don't have an inkling."

"What, Vivee?" Mac asked. "What are you talking about?"

"Oh! I forgot to tell you that we saw Martha Simmons at the fairgrounds."

"Aunt Martha?" he asked. "What was she still doing out there?"

"Who knows?" Miss Vivee said.

"She told us she had to collect her things," I said and frowned at Miss Vivee. "And she met one of her customers out there. Don't you remember?"

"Oh Lord," Miss Vivee said. "Don't go acting like I'm crazy again. "Of course I remember." She turned to Mac. "But what got me was her granddaughter."

"Marigold?" Mac asked.

"How did you know her name?" Miss Vivee asked.

"I saw her there with Martha when they tried to accost Logan."

Miss Vivee hit the table with her palm and said, "Well, she did it again."

"Martha tried to accost Logan?"

"Not Martha, she wouldn't hurt a fly. Please try to keep up, Mac. It was her granddaughter. Iris."

"Marigold," Mac and I said.

"Well they should have named her Iris with those eyes. Anyway, she tried to best our Logan."

"Really? What happened?" Mac asked.

I listened in too. I didn't remember that happening.

"Talking about she went to Stanford and that she's a nutritionist and genie . . . genie . . . Genie what, Logan?"

"Genealogist," I said.

"Right," she said and nodded. "Couldn't spit that word out." She took another sip of tea. "But Logan straightened her out."

"I did?"

"Oh I could see in your face that you knew she was lying."

I chuckled. "I didn't say that."

"But you were thinking it."

"Only the part when she said she studied nutrition at Stanford. But I must have been confused thinking she said she'd gone to school there."

"You weren't confused. She said it. And what does a nutritionist do?" Miss Vivee asked.

"A nutritionist is an expert in food, Vivee," Mac said. "They know all about it, what's healthy, what's not."

"Oh, I know what a nutritionist is," Miss Vivee waved her hand. "I'm saying compared to Logan being an archaeologist, what's a nutritionist? Logan is the re-creator of our history. She digs it up, and she tells everyone what happened thousands of years ago, and what to think. She has influence on the story of our whole world, all the way from day one."

Sounded like she had been talking to my mother. Those were almost her exact words when describing our profession. But it did make me smile to think Miss Vivee thought highly of me, or at least what I did. Sometimes I wasn't even sure if she liked me. I chuckled.

"What's funny, Missy," Miss Vivee said.

"Nothing," I said and turned my attention to studying the menu.

Viola Rose reappeared and fished a pen out of her nest of hair piled on top of her head, and an order pad out of her apron pocket. She stood poised to take our order, but said instead, "So y'all here to solve Jack Wagner's murder?"

"I say," Miss Vivee said. "Whatever gave you such an idea?"

"That's what y'all do, ain't it?" She looked around the table at us. "So, you think you can solve it?"

"His wife said he had a heart attack," Miss Vivee offered.

"Ain't that a hoot? I wouldn't be surprised if that cheating woman wasn't the murderer herself."

Miss Vivee gave me a nod, as if to say, I told you so.

"I'm not so sure if I can solve this one," Miss Vivee spoke to Viola Rose.

"I heard there was a note," Viola Rose said. "They gave you a copy?"

"You heard right," Miss Vivee said. "There is a note, and they gave me a copy."

"What you make of it?" Viola Rose asked.

"Nothing yet," Miss Vivee said.

"Well, I know you'll figure it out, Miss Vivee." Viola Rose placed her hand on Miss Vivee's shoulder. "You got a keen eye, and a mind like a steel trap. Nobody better to get the answers."

Miss Vivee blushed. "You think I'll solve it, huh?" she asked Viola Rose. "Catch the murderer?"

"I know ya will," Viola Rose said. "They'd have to put on an extra coat of grease to slide by you, Miss Vivee." She smiled then looked and Mac and me. "And your little posse." She nodded her head as if she said all she needed to say. "So what y'all having?"

"Me and Logan'll have the egg salad," Miss Vivee said. "And I'll have a cup of your split pea soup."

"Gotcha," Viola Rose said.

I don't know why she always orders for me.

"I'll have the open-face turkey sandwich, Viola Rose," I said and handed her my menu. "No egg salad."

"You want smashed taters with that?" she asked.

"Yep," I said. "With lots of gravy."

"What about Mac, Miss Vivee? You ordering for him, too?"

"No," Miss Vivee said sounding surprised that Viola Rose would ask her that. "He can order for himself."

"I think I'll have a cup of chili," Mac said.

"Chili?" Miss Vivee said. "It's hotter than the dickens outside.

"You ordered soup," I said.

She narrowed her eye at me. "Plus, it'll give you heartburn," she said turning to Mac.

"What do you suggest, Vivee?" Mac asked.

"Well, the chicken fried chicken looks good."

Viola Rose chuckled and collected the menus from Mac and Miss Vivee. "Chicken fried chicken it is."

Chapter Sixteen

"I just don't know about those flowers, Mac." Miss Vivee said. We had been eating quietly for a few minutes, and now Miss Vivee spoke in between bites.

He touched her hand. "Well, you found them all, right? Camren Wagner had them all, didn't she?"

"Yes. I told you that." Miss Vivee shook her head and took a sip of iced tea through her straw. "I mean which one? Which one of those flowers did it?"

"My question is why no one else died," I said. "They were all sick enough. And how did something get in all that food?"

"You double-checked each one of the flowers on the note?" Mac asked.

"Yes, I did," Miss Vivee. "Not that I had to, I already knew about each of them. I know all about how they poison. And from what I know, I can't say that it was any of them."

"What about smell?" Mac said. "Does anyone of them leave a smell?"

"A smell?" Miss Vivee asked.

"You mean like a fragrance," I asked swiping my turkey and bread through the last of the gravy. "A flower smell?"

"No," Mac said. "When I examined him, I smelled almonds. Now mind you it was just a prelim-"

"Almonds?" Miss Vivee's interrupted him, her face lit up. "You know what that is?" She seemed to scold him.

"Yes, I do. But I didn't know if one of those flowers would cause that smell."

"Why didn't you tell me that before?"

"We didn't talk about that," he said. "We just talked about the plants, all the flowers on the note and in your garden."

"That makes a difference, you know?" Miss Vivee said. She looked at Mac.

"I know," he said and looked back at her. "Well, at least I know now."

"And you're sure? He smelled like almonds?"

Mac closed his eyes momentarily and nodded. "I'm sure." He looked at Miss Vivee. "Positive."

"Well," Miss Vivee said and seemed to sit up a little straighter. It appeared like an anxiousness that was bottled up in her had left. "There were those fruit trees at the arboretum." Nodding, a grin on her face, she locked eyes with Mac.

Then he smiled.

"Fruit trees?" I said. "Okay." I saw how they were looking at each other. "That evidently means something to the two of you."

"What kind of fruit trees, Vivee?" Mac asked.

"I can't remember them all, but there was plum, apple, and peach." Miss Vivee tapped him on his arm.

The had an amused look on their faces. I knew they had figured it out.

"You know what that says about that note then, don't you, Vivee," Mac said and grinned.

She nodded her head. "I sure do."

"What does it mean?" I asked. I felt so out of the loop.

"That it's a red herring," Miss Vivee said.

"A red herring?" I said. "Someone went to all the trouble to make that rhyming clue and it means nothing?" I frowned up my face. "That doesn't make sense."

"Murder doesn't make sense," Mac said.

I waved my hand at them. "Okay. Get back to the fruit trees," I said. "Tell me, because I know you two have figured out how Jack Wagner died."

"Cyanide poisoning," they said in unison.

"Oh yeah," I said. "Because cyanide grows on trees. Fruit trees to be exact."

"Right," Mac said, seemingly not even recognizing the tenor of sarcastic doubt laced in my voice.

"Yes, it does," Miss Vivee echoed his affirmation.

I fell back in my seat and took in a breath. No need to argue with them, these two knew things that others, people learned enough to be Nobel scholars, could only hope to know. I just needed them to explain it to me.

"So, you wanna explain it to me?"

"Amygdalin," Miss Vivee said.

"And what is that?" I said knowing I needed to look it up.

But before I could whip out my phone, Mac told me to "Gaggle it, you'll see."

"Google, Mac. And I am, see?" I held up my cell phone. "How is it spelled?" I said more to myself than to Mac or Miss Vivee. "Ah-mig," I said sounding it out. "A-M-I-G" I typed in.

"A-M-Y," Mac corrected.

"G-D-A-L-I-N . . ." Miss Vivee's voice trailed away as she finished spelling the word.

"I got it," I said and looked up at Miss Vivee. Her face had gone white. "What's wrong?"

"A-M-Y-G-D-A-L-I-N," she said the letters slowly. And then her eyes darted from me, to Mac, and then down to her purse. She reached inside of it and pulled out the copy of the note from the food fair. It was still covered in plastic and it rattled as she held it - her hands were shaking.

"What is it, Vivee?" Mac asked.

"Those are the names of the flowers," she said.

"What?" I said and frowned. "How is that the name of the flowers?"

"Nightshade, Iris, Moleplant, Yellow Jessamine, Goldenseal, Angel's Trumpet, Delphinium,

Aconitum, and Lily of the Valley." Miss Vivee read the names of the flowers from the poem.

She pulled out her notepad and a pencil, licking the tip before she began writing. She copied the flower names from the paper. Then she wrote "AMYGDALIN" across the top. "Aconitum," she said and crossed off the "A." She continued, "Moleplant, that's the 'M.' 'Y' is Yellow Jessamine, 'G' is Goldenseal . . ."

"Oh my goodness," I said. I could already see, even before she finished, that the first letter of each flower name spelled *amygdalin*.

"An acronym," Mac said and nodded his head. He bent in closer and watched her work.

"An acronym that's already a word," Miss Vivee said as she wrote.

"So maybe the note isn't a red herring," I said.

"No. Maybe not," Miss Vivee said. "But none of those flowers on there could have killed that man. I knew that when Mac said he smelled almonds."

"You knew it already," I said, remembering her frustration earlier. "That's why you seemed troubled, and didn't know immediately what Jack Wagner died from."

She stopped writing, looked at me and smiled. "Yes, that's right. None of the flowers would have made him look like he looked when they showed me his body. Finding out about the almond smell just confirms it."

Abby L. Vandiver

"So you get to cross your name off the suspect list," I said.

"I never put it on there," Miss Vivee said with a smirk.

Well don't that just beat all, I thought and chuckled to myself. She had put me and Renmar's name on her little list, #1 suspects to be exact on Oliver and Aaron's murders as if she believed we were capable of it.

Even at her age, I knew for a fact that Miss Vivee was more capable of murder than anyone else I knew.

Chapter Seventeen

I decided to go ahead and look up the amygdalin while she finished matching them up. She was moving way too slow for me.

"Amygdalin," I read the Wikipedia entry off my cell phone, "is a poisonous cyanogenic glycoside found in many plants, but most notably in the seeds (kernels) of apricot (known as bitter almonds), peach, and plum.'" I looked up at Miss Vivee, she was still matching the flowers to the word. Mac was watching her every move.

I went back to reading and found that cyanogenic glycosides are broken down by an enzyme in the body when ingested into cyanide, glucose and benzaldehyde.

Then I found a medical reference.

"Mac," I said getting his attention. "Listen to this," I read the next paragraph. "It says here that 'Since the early 1950s, both amygdalin and a modified form named laetrile have been promoted as an alternative cancer treatment.'"

Miss Vivee interrupted me. "That's hogwash," she said without lifting her eyes up from the page she was writing on.

"Well, this guy on here," I looked back at my phone. "National arm wrestling champion, Jason Vale said eating apricot kernels cured him of kidney and pancreatic cancer."

"*Pfft*," Miss Vivee blew out.

I laughed and clicked off my search to look for apricot kernels. "Oh my gosh!" I said. "Amazon sells apricot seeds. Bitter Almonds. Look." I held up my phone and Miss Vivee glanced up at it before going back to her writing. "It must not be too bad," I continued. "Otherwise they couldn't sell it. How does it work?" I swiped my phone to Google it.

"B17." Miss Vivee clicked her tongue. "But there's no such thing."

"Yeah?" I asked. "Let's see what this says." I clicked back through my searches and returned to the Wikipedia article. "Where was I . . . Oh." I found the paragraph about cancer treatment. "Okay. '. . . it is promoted as an alternative cancer treatment, often using the *misnomer*,'" I emphasized, "'Vitamin B17.'" Miss Vivee was right. I looked up at her. She had taken out her suspect notebook and was scrawling away, paying no attention to me.

"'But studies have found them,'" I went back to reading, "'to be clinically *ineffective* in the treatment of cancer, as well as potentially toxic or lethal when taken by mouth, due to-'" I chuckled and read the last words, "'cyanide poisoning.'"

I lifted my head as I finished reading and found Miss Vivee staring at me.

"Told you, Missy," she said.

"Soooo," I said putting the puzzle pieces that we had together. "You think Jack Wagner ate some kernels from . . ." I looked back at the Wikipedia page, "an apricot, peach or plum, ingested amygdalin, and then died from cyanide poisoning?"

"I don't *think* that's what happened," Miss Vivee said tucking her notebook and pencils down in her purse. "I know it is. That's why I added all three of them from the arboretum to my suspect list. "

"Three of them?" I said scrunching my nose. "Who?"

"Camren Wagner. Her boyfriend, Robert Bernard-"

"Wait," I said. "You don't know that guy was her boyfriend."

"You heard Viola Rose. And that man didn't fool me one little bit," Miss Vivee said. "He was slicker than snot on a glass door knob. Every time he opened his mouth, he told a lie." She shook her head. "Windy as a sack full of farts."

I tried to picture that.

Then I shook my head wanting to dismiss the thought. "That doesn't mean they were dating," I said.

"I'd bet a fat man on it."

Miss Vivee had a penchant for placing bets on fat men. I wonder did she ever win any of those bets.

"Who's the third person?" I asked getting back on track. "You said 'all three,' who else?"

"That Gavin Tanner."

I raised my eyebrows and chuckled. "He was so nice to you. Why would you think he'd kill anybody?"

"Don't know the why, just yet, but I know he works at a place where the murder weapon is in abundance, and he was at the fair. That's means and opportunity." She glanced at me. "Plus, he seemed kind of nervous."

"He did not," I said, although he did fidget, but I took that to be because of Miss Vivee.

"Did to me. Nervous as a long tail cat on a porch of rocking chairs," Miss Vivee said and turned her head catching Viola Rose's eye. She beckoned to her.

"He had the 'means' only if it really was cyanide poisoning that killed Jack Wagner," I said without too much conviction. I don't know why I even bothered to argue the point, she and Mac were always right.

"It fits," Mac said agreeing with Ms. Vivee. "Like I said, I smelled a faint scent of almonds when I took a look at him."

"That just sounds crazy to me," I said. "Not you smelling the almonds," I directed my eyes to Mac, then back to Miss Vivee. "I just don't understand how such a common food could be so deadly? People eat peaches and plums all the time."

"They don't eat the seeds," Miss Vivee said.

"That's right, normally, they don't," Mac said.

"And it's what's inside of the kernel that contains the poison," Miss Vivee added.

"That's true." Mac nodded. "Swallowing the pit whole ain't so bad, it's when you get what's inside. And you'd have to eat a lot of it for it to kill you."

"How much?" I said and swiped the face of my iPhone. I needed to Google that, too.

"Y'all ready for ya check?" Viola Rose asked when she came over to the table.

"No, I was thinking I'd have some of your peach cobbler," Miss Vivee said. "All this talk of fruit Logan's been doing has made my mouth water."

"You want a scoop of vanilla ice cream with that?" Viola Rose asked.

"Mmmm. That's sounds good," Miss Vivee said. "And bring some for Mac and Logan, too."

"No thank you," I said looking up from my Google search. "None for me. I don't know that I'll ever eat peaches again."

"Oh phooey," Miss Vivee said and waved her hand at me. "I'll take a cup of coffee with it, too."

"You can bring me another cup, too," Mac said. "But this time, make mine decaf."

"Gotcha," I heard Viola Rose say as I went back to my poison, common fruit search.

"Here," I said. "It says that it would take about 100 grams of peach seed, which contains about 88mg of cyanide to be dangerous. And each pit yields about 10 grams." I looked up. "It says that it would take somewhere between 13 to 15 raw peach pit kernels to be in the lethal range for an average sized adult."

"See, so even if Gus dropped a few peach kernels in the cobbler, it wouldn't kill you," Miss Vivee said.

I wasn't sure if she was being sarcastic or not.

"Doesn't take as many cherries, though," she said.

"Did you see cherry trees, Vivee?" Mac asked.

"Not a one," she said.

But I'd seen cherry pie.

And a lot of sick people.

My heart rate quickened, and a chill ran over my arms.

I Googled cherries.

It read: "Hydrogen cyanide is lethal at about 1.52 milligrams per kilogram."

I looked up from my reading, and closed my eyes. "Okay, if I convert that from milligrams to grams, just to make the units easier to work with," I mumbled. "And rounding it off, 1.52 milligrams is about 0.002 grams, let me see . . ..002 grams for every kilogram a person weighed . . ." I looked back down at my phone. "Okay. And a hundred and fifty pound person weighs . . ." I stared down at the floor and did the math. "About sixty-eight kilograms. So then, if I multiply 68 times .002, it would take about 0.136 grams of cherry pits to kill a 150lb person." I nodded my head, satisfied with my calculations.

I went back to the website on my phone and found the place I had left off. It said that "a single cherry yields roughly 0.17 grams of cyanide per gram of seed."

I didn't need to do the math on that.

Crap!

It would only take the inside of one and a half, or at the most, two cherry pits to kill someone.

"Oh my, Lord," I said under my breath.

"What are you mumbling about, Logan," Miss Vivee voice floated past my ears.

Could that be what made all the cherry pie eaters sick? I shook my head. *Couldn't be*, I thought.

"How do the pits taste?" I asked Miss Vivee and Mac.

"Pits?" Miss Vivee asked.

"Fruit pits from the ones that contain cyanogenic glycoside."

"Bitter," Mac said.

"But this cobbler is sweet," Miss Vivee said taking in a mouthful. "The only thing you might get from this is a cavity." She swallowed the pie and took a sip of her coffee.

"Or fat," Mac said.

"You think I'm fat," Miss Vivee asked, sitting down her coffee cup. She looked down at herself and smoothed her hand down her front.

"Never," Mac said and winked at her. "You're perfect any way you are."

Those two were too sweet for me, probably even more so than that cobbler. But cavities or fat wasn't what was bothering me.

I typed in "cyanide poisoning symptoms."

I found my answer on *eMedicine Health*. It relayed the symptoms as "general weakness, confusion, bizarre behavior, excessive sleepiness, coma, shortness of breath, headache, dizziness, and seizures." I shook my head.

I don't remember any of that.

I skipped to the next paragraph. "An acute ingestion," it read, "will have a dramatic, rapid onset, immediately affecting the heart and causing sudden collapse."

They did collapse.

I read the next paragraph. "The skin of a cyanide-poisoned person can sometimes be unusually pink or cherry-red because oxygen will stay in the blood and not get into the cells. The person may also breathe very fast and have either a very fast or very slow heartbeat."

And they were pink . . .

I looked over at Miss Vivee. She was eating her cobbler, and talking to Mac. Enjoying her afternoon. Pleased with herself, I knew, for figuring out how Jack Wagner died after the note had stumped her. But, Miss Vivee had given no never mind to *all* the people who got sick. All she concentrated on was the one who died.

So, what did make everyone else sick?

Was it the kernels that killed Jack Wagner?

And if so, what kind of kernels killed Jack Wagner? Plum. Peach. Cherry?

Each one of those kernel didn't contain cyanide, I reasoned. They contained cyanogenic glycoside, which the body breaks down into cyanide once ingested. What about if they didn't take in enough of it? Then the body couldn't make enough cyanide to kill them. It would just make them sick.

I thought about it. Each one of those kernel does contain amygdalin, though. I let my eyes roll up. Whichever fruit was used, if a fruit was used . . . I brought my eyes back down and looked at Miss Vivee . . . whichever fruit was used contained amygdalin.

I typed "symptoms of amygdalin poisoning" in the search box on my phone. The first link I clicked on listed thirty of them.

Abdominal pain, sweating, vomiting, weakness, bluish skin . . .

Mild poisoning also included chest tightness, and muscle weakness, it read.

I thought back to all the blue faces, and then to that man clutching his chest. I remembered when Mac and I had left the pie tent, I saw a line of people waiting for the Porta potties. One woman who the medics had found lying flat on the ground, was being hoisted up on a gurney. She was too weak to stand. And then there was that gentlemen seated in a wooden chair near the tent his ear of corn limp in his hand. I glanced back down at my phone. They all had the symptoms.

That's it, I thought. *Had to be.*

Whoever gave Jack Wagner amygdalin, had also sprinkled a little of it on food all over the fair. He got enough for it to turn into a lethal dose cyanide, they didn't.

If that was possible.

And how did they do that?

Why did they do that?

"The murderer wasn't trying to frame someone else for this murder," I said in an unexpected outburst. I hadn't meant to be so loud, it was just the realization startled me.

"What in the world are you talking about," Miss Vivee said and frowned.

"The note," I said.

"What do you mean, Logan?" Mac asked.

"Miss Vivee thought she needed to prove that she didn't kill Jack Wagner because she had all the flowers."

"Jack Wagner wasn't poisoned by any of the flowers on the note," Miss Vivee said.

"Exactly," I said. "But I think that note is more than a red herring, it's really a clue to who the killer is."

"Of course it is," Miss Vivee said. "The killer wrote it."

"They wrote it to frame someone else," Mac said.

"To take the suspicion off of themselves," Miss Vivee added.

"No I think they want us – rather Miss Vivee – to figure out who they are."

"Who is who?"

"Who the killer is," I said. "Think about it, whoever killed Jack Wagner gave us a clue in a poem, and then made everyone else sick. They made a big production number out of it."

"That's not right," Miss Vivee said. "The murderer couldn't expect anyone to figure it out from that poem, because nothing in it pointed to the right clues to follow. Nobody was killed by a botanical poison."

"And why would the killer want to be caught?" Mac asked.

Chapter Eighteen

"When we leave here," Miss Vivee said as we waited for Viola Rose to come back with Mac's change and her to-go order of peach cobbler. "We've got to find the Sheriff."

I really think she only ordered cobbler to irritate me.

"I know that you're not going to tell him about your list of suspects," I said.

"No," she said and nothing more.

Again with the one word answer. That made me think she was up to something.

"Well," I said. "What are you going to tell him?"

"About the cause of death."

"They sent out a toxicology request when they did the autopsy." I said. "Bay told me that they were still waiting for the results. I mean it's nothing wrong with telling him, but they'll find out soon enough on their own."

"They won't look for cyanide," Mac said. "It's not part of a routine toxicology screen in an autopsy."

"So you're going to tell the sheriff that it was amygdaline?"

"Of course I am." She glanced at me. "Why is that surprising to you?"

"Because you never want to tell anybody, anything until you've figured out the whole thing," I said. You know you like the shock and awe of the reveal. Quite the show-off, if you ask me."

"I am not," she said and jutted out her chin. "And no one asked you. Plus, this is different. The Sheriff asked me to help." She nodded. "They need to know to look for cyanide, otherwise, if they don't check for it now they'd have to exhume the body later."

With that she huffed and scooted herself out of the booth. Mac waved at Viola Rose to keep the change and followed behind Miss Vivee. We loaded into my Jeep and I took Mac back home before we headed back to the Maypop.

"How was your doctor's appointment?" Renmar asked as soon as we walked in the door.

"What?" Miss Vivee said.

"The doctor in Augusta," Renmar said and then looked at me. "You did go, didn't you?"

I'd nearly forgotten we'd gone.

"We went," I said.

"You two had been gone so long, I started to get worried."

"Here," Miss Vivee said and wagged the card in front of her face. "They said I needed more help than they could offer in one day, so I have to go back."

"Oh my," Renmar said and put her hand on her cheek. "Logan, is something wrong with Momma?"

I'd never heard Renmar call Miss Vivee "Momma" before, she always said "Mother." She must've been really concerned, which was understandable. But I didn't know how to make it better because Miss Vivee wasn't being truthful with her.

Maybe I should just tell her what really happened.

"No need of asking Logan," Miss Vivee said. "I went in by myself, she doesn't know what happened."

"What did happen?" There was an uneasiness in Renmar's voice.

Miss Vivee looked at Renmar. I saw a flash of concern in her face for upsetting her daughter. "Nothing, Renmar. And there's nothing wrong with me. They gave me a clean bill of health."

"So why did they give you another appointment?" Renmar seemed confused.

"They didn't," Miss Vivee said and smiled. "I made the appointment for you.' She pushed the card into Renmar.

"Mother!"

"I've had a long day," Miss Vivee said and waved her hand. "I'm going to bed."

Renmar flapped her hands down on her side with a loud *thump!* And looked at me.

"I didn't go in with her Renmar."

"Well, you were supposed to be watching her."

"They told me to stay put. You know, I'm not related – yet and they're just not going to share information about her with me."

"That's why I should have gone," she said.

"Well, she did make you an appointment . . ."

"You know Mother wasn't all this trouble until you got here."

Oh here we go.

"I'm going to my room, too," I said and headed up the stairs before she could say anything else.

I got upstairs, thinking it was way too early for bed, even though I was tired from the harrowing day with the Dotage Dynamic Duo, and there, sitting on my bed was Miss Vivee.

"I thought you were going to bed?" I said.

"It's the middle of the day." She looked at me like I was crazy.

I just shook my head.

"Where's your phone," she reached out her hand. "I need to call the Sheriff."

I handed her the phone. I knew she couldn't use it.

She took it, turned it over a couple of times, looked at the black screen and back up at me. "How do you turn this thing on?"

I reached over and pressed down the button on the front of the phone, my lock screen came up. She started pressing numbers, then she put the phone up to her ear. She pulled it back and looked at it. She gave it a shake and put it back up to her ear.

"Does this thing work?"

"Give it here," I said. I sat down on the bed next to her. "Do you know the number?"

"Of course I do," she said and rattled it off.

I unlocked the phone and dialed the number she gave me.

"Give it here," she said and wiggled her fingers in front of my face. "Let me talk."

And talk she did. I'd put the speaker on so I could hear the other end of the conversation, and Miss Vivee herself was turned on loud. She yelled at the phone and told the Sheriff that those flowers in the poem on that note had nothing to do with the murder, but that his wife had all those flowers in her garden.

Then she told him that Jack Wagner had been killed by cyanide poisoning, and that it was probably from the kernel of one of the peach, apple or plum trees at the arboretum. And she must have told him three times in their five minute conversation that the ME would have to do a special test to check for the poison. He thanked her and told her that he would call Bay, and let him know what she found out. She said, "Good. You tell him everything I've told you. He needs to hear it from you. That's why I called you."

"Well that's good to know Miss Vivee. Because it sure wasn't a heart attack that killed Jackson Wagner," Sheriff Haynes said. "Just got the autopsy report back and the coroner said he'd been fit as a fiddle."

"Well you'd thought it was poison at first sight," Miss Vivee said. "Just proving you're getting an eye for these things."

"Unfortunately, it looks like I am."

They hung up and she said, "Call Bay. Let's tell him what I found out."

"Thought you wanted the Sheriff to tell him."

"Haven't you learned anything from me?" she asked.

"I've learned you lie a lot."

"Well, that's a start," Miss Vivee said and nodded her head. "And if you stick with me, Kiddo. You'll learn a lot more."

We called Bay and Miss Vivee shouted at him through the phone the same information that she had shouted to Sheriff Haynes. He got off saying that he had a call coming in from the Sheriff, but not before warning us not to get involved.

"Too late," Miss Vivee leaned into the phone and yelled. "We're in up to our elbows."

I got Miss Vivee out of my room, pulled out my laptop and laid across the bed. I hadn't forgotten how Camren Wagner looked at me when Miss Vivee put on two pairs of glasses. No one would ever think I didn't take good care of Miss Vivee again. So, I Googled "eyeglass frames at Walmart," and there were seven pages of them. Some sold by other manufacturers and shipped to Walmart, and some available for immediate pick-up in the store. I limited my choices to those I could pick up, then I picked out a few that I thought Miss Vivee would like.

I had to see Renmar again to get Miss Vivee's ophthalmologist's number, but I didn't stick around long after she gave it to me. Not even long enough to answer her questions on why I needed it. I called her doctor and had them fax her eye prescription to the Walmart up in Augusta where the frames would be. Thank goodness Miss Vivee had recently had an eye exam.

That done, I carried my open laptop down the hall to Miss Vivee's room to show her.

"Which pair do you like best?" I said.

She squinted at the screen for a minute then pushed it away. "You pick them out," she said.

"They're for you," I countered. "Why would I choose a pair?"

"I'm happy with the pair I have."

You don't have a pair, I said to myself. *You have two.* But I wasn't going to let her dour demeanor detour me.

Although she complained about "spending good money" on the pair of prescription sunglasses, I knew it wasn't that because she had no problem whipping out her American Express Blue card at a moment's notice. And right now it didn't matter the reason, I was going to get her a pair.

"Fine." I padded back down to my room, fell onto the bed, and clicked on the pair I thought best. I felt like Robert Bernard determining the appropriate one for her, which turned out to be harder to do than I originally thought.

Maybe he was a pretty smart guy . . .

After I entered my credit card information and everything was ordered, I called Walmart to make sure they received the fax, and to let them know which frames went with the prescription for Vivienne Pennywell (I wondered if I should put "Caspard" in there somewhere). The optician told me I could pick them up the next day.

I hung up the phone very pleased with myself. I smiled knowing I was the one that had made sure Miss Vivee would finally stop wearing two pairs of glasses.

Then my smile faded. *I've turned into Renmar*, I thought. Making Miss Vivee do something that she didn't want to do just because I thought it was right.

Crap.

Chapter Nineteen

After I finished ordering Miss Vivee's glasses, I decided to take a look at the flowers in the poem. The author's (rather murderer's) description told me the color and shape of some, but Mac had made me realize that I didn't even know a lily when I saw it.

Just as I finished looking at the last one, Bay called. He said he'd pick me up at seven to take me to a nice restaurant. He wanted to give me something.

That's when I felt the first butterfly hit.

Then they went full force, and my stomach was all a-flutter. And they somehow must've gotten into my head because my temples started to ache. I had to stand still, clutching my chest, and catch my breath.

This is it!

He *was* going to give me a proper proposal.

I knew he had wanted to speak to my parents and although I was nearly thirty years old, I appreciated his consideration. But, I hadn't heard from my parents yet, so his invite to dinner took me by surprise. I had figured at least my mother would have called me to let me know she'd spoken to him. Maybe they were waiting until I officially got the ring. He must've told them how he was planning on taking me out tonight. I smiled. I'll call them when we get back.

I jumped up off the bed. I couldn't wait. But I knew I needed something to wear, so I decided to drive up to Augusta. I bathed and washed my hair. Then I let Miss Vivee know I was leaving so she wouldn't come looking for me.

I got directions from Google Map and went to the Dillard's on Wrightsboro Road, just down from the Walmart where I'd ordered Miss Vivee's glasses.

At least tomorrow I'll know right where to go.

I turned into the mall and parked my car. After wandering around the store for ten minutes trying to find the Misses Department, I perused through several racks and found that I really didn't know how to find a dress to fit the occasion. I hadn't ever been the girly type, spending my days playing in the dirt and the sun, I was a jeans and tennis shoes kind of girl. But, tonight, I wanted to look nice. Really nice. *Maybe even pretty*. I smiled at the thought until I walked past a mirror and caught my reflection.

Okay, maybe not pretty, I thought as I ran my hands through my naturally curly hair.

After announcing to the store clerk that I was getting engaged, I had everyone in earshot trying to help me find the "right" dress. Shoppers had stopped what they were doing and were giving the store clerk dresses for me to try on. When I stepped out the dressing room in a soft pink, short sleeved sheath dress, everyone ooo'd and awed, agreeing it was the one.

The midi dress with small appliqué flowers all over had a pink ribbon band around its empire waist, and once on it made me feel like a princess.

"This is it," I said as I turned from side to side in the mirror. I did feel pretty.

I thanked everyone for their help and headed to the shoe department, a couple of the dress department shoppers in tow. We all decided on a pair of kitten heel pumps with a buckle closure. The pearl-gold, pointed closed-toe pumps had rhinestone studs on the straps hat made it seem as if the whole shoe sparkled. Then one woman practically dragged me down the mall to the Mac store and had them make up my face.

Swinging my new shoes by the handle of the white plastic bag with one hand, carrying my new dress in a garment bag with the other, and the thrill of my quickly approaching engagement swirling around in my head, I practically skipped out to my jeep. Filled with enough happy thoughts to consume every fiber of my being I hopped in my car, but as soon as I turned the ignition, for some odd reason, that stupid poem popped into my head and I couldn't think.

Geesh.

I pulled out the parking lot and onto I-520 headed back to the Maypop to get ready. I wanted to flat iron my hair, and that would take time. But those words from that stupid poem were swimming around in my mind.

Fair flowers of the field . . .

I turned up the radio.

Mystery and wonder they provide . . .

I changed the radio station. Katie Perry's *Roar* was on. Good, I love this song.

But the Lily of the Valley that one's the most grande . . .

Crap.

I turned the music all the way up and shouted the words to the song. But no matter how loud the radio, or my bad singing got, those darn words were doing flips and making waves in my brain clouding it so much that I thought it was going to burst.

I took in a breath and blew it out my mouth. Okay. Fine. I'll think about this.

So. If amygdaline killed Jack Wagner and made all those people sick, then why put the flowers on the note? They had to mean something. And, why try to frame Miss Vivee, if that's what they were doing? Or, if not, then as Mac said, why do something to get caught? They'd have to know that planning a murder is a capital offense, and that Georgia had the death penalty. I shook my head. Mac was right, no one would want to get caught.

So then why the references to the flowers?

The trickery and deception that draws one near . . .

Yep. Okay. You got me.

I turned down the volume on the radio, and took the off ramp two exits before the one for Yasamee.

Those flowers at the fairground were certainly "drawing" me near.

Come see me . . . they were saying. So I was going to see them. Again.

As soon as I got to the sign for Lincoln Park, the flowers came into view. I slowed down and took them in. I had planned on parking and walking through the fields. I wanted to find those lilies. I had seared into my mind a picture of each of the nine flowers in that poem, (and a bunch of other poison flowers just in case I ever came into contact with them) and I had decided to double check that none of the other flower were there. It was not probable, but certainly possible, that Miss Vivee had missed something, especially since after running into Aunt Martha, we hadn't looked at any flowers.

But I didn't get a chance to get an up-close look at anything because, there in the field, digging in the dirt, was Gavin Tanner.

What in the world is he doing?

I slowed down even more and tried to see what he was up to. He had a trowel and a basket filled with flowers, and every few feet, he'd dig in the dirt and pull up a flower from the root, and throw it on the pile. I had come to a complete stop as I watched him. Then, still bent over a flower, he must've heard a horn that honked for me to get out of the way because he looked up and saw me. At least I think he saw me. Slowly standing up, I noticed a little grin spread across his face.

Oh crap!
I sped off, but I knew it was too late.

ƐƷƐƷƐƷƐƷƐƷƐƷƐƷƐƷ

"The Frog Hollow Tavern?" I said to Bay as we parked in front of it. It sure didn't sound like a romantic restaurant to me. "This is where we're going?"

"Yeah, babe. This is one of the fancier and more modern spots in Downtown Augusta. Plus, I thought it'd make you feel more at home."

Why would he think that?

I stepped inside and looked around. The restaurant itself was spacious. There was an air of coziness but not romance. At least to me. There was a large, wooden full-sized bar, a small seating area with a couch and a few chairs to the right of it, and two loveseats on the opposite side of the room. The restaurant looked like the cellar of a Spanish tavern – long wooden custom made wine shelves covered the walls.

I stood by while Bay checked our reservation and then leaned over and whispered something in the hostess' ear.

He must be setting up for his one-knee proposal.

I started smiling.

"What you so happy about?" he asked.

I shook my head. "Nothing."

I saw a huge blackboard with the night's specials written across it as we followed our hostess as she weaved us through small rooms to our seat, and my mouth started to water.

Everyone on the wait staff smiled at us as we passed.

Maybe they know about the proposal, too.

We got to our seat, Bay pulled my chair out for me and the hostess put the menus on the table. I looked around and then up. Our table seemed overly lit, making me feel pretty exposed.

I'm going to be so embarrassed when he gives me that ring.

I did have to admit, though, that the place smelled heavenly, and we didn't have to wait long before someone came to get our order. They arrived with drinks.

"I ordered that for you, Baby," Bay said. "It's their signature drink."

"Looks good," I said. "What is it?" I took a sip.

"It a Tea Hive," Bay said

"Oh. My." I closed my eyes. This is so good. It's the best cocktail I ever had. What's in it?" I asked and took another sip.

"It's a wonderful concoction of honeysuckle vodka, chamomile, lemon, and honey," the waiter said. "We're pretty famous for it."

"I can see why. I love it," I said and smiled.

"You know what you want to eat?" Bay asked me.

"Yep," I nodded, and dabbed my mouth with my napkin. "Do you?"

"Yeah. But let me order an appetizer for us to share. I want you to try it, okay?"

I smiled. "Okay."

Bay smiled up at the waiter. "We'll have the House Smoked Andouille Sausage." He looked at me. "It has a strong smoky flavor," he explained. "I think you'll like it."

"Yes, it does," the waiter took over the explanation. "And it's served on a bed of Anson Mills' Organic Grits with Caramelized Vidalia Onions on top, and it comes with a small dab of the Tavern Mustard on the side." The waiter and Bay licked their lips.

"Okay, I'm convinced. Bring it on," I said.

They both laughed.

"Good," the waiter said, noting our appetizer on his order pad. "And what will you have for an entrée ma'am."

I ordered the double pork chop. The waiter had explained that it was brined over three days, *sou vide*, then pan seared in butter and roasted over sweet potatoes.

Bay ordered the Florida Gulf Day Boat Red Snapper. It was laid out on a bed of Chal's corn, red bell peppers, Vidalia onions, celery and pulled Parsley leaves. Combined with a House Pickled Sweet Onion Butter. He added to that a side of their Smoked Gouda Mac 'n Cheese.

So many onions, I thought, *I might not want to kiss him when he gives me that ring.*

Abby L. Vandiver

I giggled.

"You sure are giddy tonight."

"Am not."

Our meal came in short order and there was a mountain of food. I reached my fork across the table, and flaked off a small piece of Bay's fish. I slid the fork past my lips and it melted in my mouth. It was so good. Moist and tender, every flavor from its fresh vegetables bed came through.

"I should have gotten that," I said.

"You haven't even tasted yours," he said.

So I took the knife to cut a piece of the pork and it sliced through it like it was butter, the meat fell off the center bone. I put a piece in my mouth, and then another, shoveling sweet potatoes in after that.

"Omigosh," I said, jaws full of food. "This is soooo good."

We ate in silence, but my thoughts were going a mile a minute. I wondered how he was going to do it. Would everyone stop eating and look at us? Would I cry?

"You want dessert?" Bay asked as I finished my last bite.

"No," I said. "I'm full." If he only knew, I barely made it through dinner trying to wait for my "gift." No way, I could get anything else down my throat. It had already started to tighten up. I took the cloth napkin off my lap and laid it on the table. "I think it's time."

"Time?" he asked. "Time for what?"

"Don't play with me boy."

He gave me one of his smirks. The kind he'd given me when we first met – me as the fugitive and him as the law.

"Don't look at me like that," I said. "I knew he was up to something. I looked down at my hand. My ring finger on my left hand to be exact. It was twitching.

"Okay, baby." He reached in his pocket and my heart stopped. Then he pulled out an envelope.

I almost fell out of the chair.

"What the heck is that?" I wanted to throw my knife at him.

"Two tickets."

"They better be honeymoon tickets with my 1 ½ carat, emerald cut ring attached to them."

He gave out a hearty laugh. "I talked to your father," he said and handed me the envelope. "And your mother, and they decided we should get engaged up there since they hadn't met me yet."

"Up where?" I asked and took the envelope.

"In Cleveland," he said.

I opened the envelope and took out the two first class tickets. Then I shook the envelope to make sure nothing else was in there. I looked at Bay.

"I'll give you the ring when we get there."

"But I bought a new dress," I pointed to it. "New shoes." I swung a foot out from under the table. "I got my face all made up, and it took me an hour to flat iron my hair."

"And you look beautiful," he said, he reached across the table and took my hand. "And that ring is going to look good on this finger."

"If I don't die of anticipation first," I said and jerked my hand away. "And order me a slice of that seven-layer chocolate decadent cake I saw on the menu."

"You want it to go?" Bay asked signaling for the waiter.

"No," I said. "I want to eat it here. And since I have to wait so long, and spend so much money just to find out I'm getting a trip to Cleveland instead of a ring," I took a gulp of my drink, "I'ma need that ring to be two carats."

Chapter Twenty

I woke up early the next morning after my fake proposal dinner, and as usual followed my nose down to the kitchen. And there, standing in the doorway, chatting it up with Renmar, was Gavin Tanner.

"Hi, Logan," he said.

What was he up to?

I mumbled a hello, and grabbed a glass and the half gallon of orange juice out the fridge. I usually ate in the kitchen, but I wasn't hanging out with him, not after yesterday when I saw him in the field. I didn't know what he was up to, but I had a feeling it wasn't something he was supposed to be doing. Plus, Miss Vivee had him pegged as a murderer.

I waved a good-bye, and went into the dining room. There were sweet rolls out, and eggs and bacon in a warmer for the breakfast crowd. I grabbed a plate, and piled it up, stopping at the fruit bar before I slid into a seat at one of the small, round tables in the corner.

I hadn't finished chewing my first mouthful when Gavin appeared in the dining area, looking around until he spotted me, he rambled over to my table.

"Hi there," he said.

"We spoke in the kitchen, remember?" I said.

"You mind if I join you?" he asked.

"You don't have any food." I bit my bacon, chewing it, and sized him up.

Could he be a murderer?

He looked around at the food, and back at me. He acted as if he wasn't quite sure if he should get something to eat or not. He cracked his knuckles and just hovered over me.

"Well?" I said.

He sat down in the seat across from me. "What were you doing at the field yesterday?" he asked and scratched his elbow.

"I should ask you that same question."

He took in a breath and ran his hand through his hair. "I was taking flowers."

"Yes, I know," I said. "I saw you. Why?" I crunched on another bite of bacon.

He let out that breath, then looked around, as if he didn't want anyone else to hear him. "They're going to dig up that field you know. Bulldoze it."

"No. I didn't know," I said. "Who is this 'they?' Robert Bernard?" I asked.

"Yes. Mr. Land Tycoon, himself." He shifted in his seat.

"Land tycoon?" I asked and chuckled. "And who is he working with, Mrs. Wagner? Because she didn't seem like the type to want to rip flowers up out of the ground to me."

He looked at me out of the corner of his eye like he was thinking. "Nah," he said after a pause. "I don't think it's her. He might have had another partner for that."

"Really, now?" I wiped my mouth with a napkin. "I thought you told me they had a thing." Then I waved my hand dismissing the conversation. I didn't want to participate in his gossip. Plus, it seemed as if he was making stuff up. "What about Mr. Wagner?" I said "Didn't he want to build the condos?"

"Oh no." He shook his head. "He had a special attachment to that land."

"Why? What was his attachment?"

"I don't know," he shrugged. "But I do know he was upset with Mrs. Wagner for allowing Mr. Bernard to hang around, especially after he found out he wanted to get a hold of the land so he could build the condos."

"How do you know that?" I asked.

"I heard Mr. Bernard and Mr. Wagner arguing. They were pretty loud."

"So?"

"So, Mr. Bernard was pretty upset. Said that the land was going to waste and that a residential subdivision would be the best use for that land."

Freckle Face with his best use analyses did share my sentiments.

"Where was Mrs. Wagner?"

"When?" he asked.

"During the argument," I said.

"Oh. I dunno."

"She wasn't there?"

"No," he shook his head and scratched the back of his neck.

"Whose side do you think she was on?"

He looked off for a minute then hunched his shoulders. "I don't know. But I do know them two always had their heads together. Mrs. Wagner and Mr. Bernard. So maybe. But I'm thinking it's that pretty young blonde that had his ear about the land."

He was starting with the gossiping again.

"What does all of this have to do with you digging up flowers?" I steered the conversation back to the real reason he had come looking for me.

"Those are expensive flowers out in that field." He looked down at his hands. "Some of them anyway."

"And so?"

"And I was just getting clippings-"

"You dug them up," I said. "You didn't clip anything."

"Yeah. That's what I meant." He rubbed his hand over his face.

"You should say what you mean." I waited for him to say something. "Well?"

"Well, I'm going to start my own greenhouse."

"And?"

"And it's expensive to start. I need those flowers. Mr. Wagner would have killed me if he knew I took any flowers from that place. A field full of exotic, expensive flowers where no one comes but once a year." He shook his head.

"So now that he's dead, you figured you'd just take them?"

"Yeah, well I didn't see the harm," he said. "I only took a few and Mrs. Wagner will probably let Mr. Bernard bulldoze that place now."

"I thought you said she wasn't in on the bulldozing part of it."

"Those two always had their heads together."

"Yeah, you said that already." I put the last bit of food in my mouth, and downed my orange juice. "Well, I have to go," I said. I got up and walked away, leaving my plate, and him at that table.

Chapter Twenty-One

Miss Vivee insisted that we go to Walmart in her car. She hated having to climb into my jeep, and I hated trying to maneuver her boat-like car over dry land. So we had a stand-off. Both of us pouting, crossing our arms, and stomping our feet.

She let out several longsuffering sighs and said, "Do you want me to die?" She flapped her arms down to her side, and tilted her head.

"Die?" I said.

"Yes," she said, her face looking weary. "I will die if I have to ride in that Jeep today."

"We'll take your car, Miss Vivee," I said. I saw the crinkle in her eye, when I gave in, happy she'd won. And I knew she'd only made that remark to get her way, but it worked. With all the death going on around me, the notion of Miss Vivee being part of it all was unsettling. I even ended up feeling sorry for giving her grief about it.

But I was sorrier that I had to drive her car.

"It's on 'E,'" I said once we were in the car, and I'd turned the ignition.

"We'll pick up Mac so he can pump the gas," Miss Vivee said.

"Mac's going with us?" I asked. I enjoyed his company, but she hadn't said anything to me about it.

"No," she said and frowned. "I don't feel like being bothered with all his sweet talking, and touchy-feely mess today. He's just going to pump the gas."

If she didn't want to see him, why even go pick him up?

"I can pump gas, Miss Vivee."

"Why should you pump gas when there's a man available?" She glanced at me. "You'll learn, they're not good for much – fixing a flat, pumping gas, taking out the trash – so you gotta let them do the things they're made for whenever possible. Plus, a man likes to think he's needed."

I shook my head and chuckled. "Don't you need Mac?" I asked.

"I need Mac like I need a hole in my head," she said, and then patted me on my hand. "But God made men as our help meet, so we're stuck with them." She nodded. "Can't live with 'em, can't kill 'em, so . . ." she raised her eyebrows and threw up her hands.

I headed over to Mac. I didn't want to have this conversation with Miss Vivee. I had chosen not to date for much of my life, but I didn't think I'd ever thought that way about men. I had a father, brother, and five uncles that had done so much more. And now, I loved having Bay around, and not just for taking out the trash either.

Abby L. Vandiver

I glanced at Miss Vivee. I knew, though, that she really didn't mean it. I knew she loved Mac, and Mac loved her. And I was sure that getting him to pump gas for us was just a ruse to see him. We pulled in front of Mac's house and I got out, went up to his front door and rang the bell.

Mac came to the door, Rover at his heels.

"Hey Mac," I said. "Miss Vivee wants you to come down to the gas station with us and pump gas."

"Okay." He didn't flinch or fuss. "Let me just grab my hat." He turned to walk away and then turned back. "Do I need to get my wallet? Does she want me to pay for it?"

I hunched my shoulders. "I dunno," I said. "She just told me to come get you so you can pump the gas."

"I'll grab it just in case," he said and limped hastily back into the house, disappearing around a corner. I went back down to the car.

"He's coming," I said. "He asked me if he needed to bring money."

"For what?" she asked.

"To pay for the gas."

"That male chauvinist pig," Miss Vivee said and clicked her tongue. "What does he think? I don't have any money?"

I laughed. "I don't think he thought that, Miss Vivee. I think he was just being nice."

"Or condescending."

"Here he comes." I watched him walk down his walkway. Even with his cane, he had a pep in his step that I knew was there because he was going to see Miss Vivee. "Be nice," I said.

"Well, aren't you looking lovely today, Vivienne," Mac said as he climbed into the backseat.

"You've seen me in this outfit a thousand times."

"And each time, I think you look even lovelier than the last time."

"Oh phooey," Miss Vivee said and to my surprise she blushed, and her dismay over him offering to pay for her gas seemingly just dissipated. "We're going to Walmart up in Augusta." She turned in her seat. "Logan's buying me a pair of prescription sunglasses. You wanna go?"

Hadn't she just told me she didn't want to be bothered with him?

"I'd enjoy that, if Logan doesn't mind."

"Of course she doesn't," Miss Vivee said and turned back in her seat. "I didn't pack any sandwiches or anything for the trip, Mac. I hope you ate."

Trip? We were going twenty-five miles up the road. All highway, it'd take fifteen – twenty minutes at the most.

"Oh, I'm fine," Mac said. "I had a piece of toast and a cup of coffee."

"Then you're just about full, huh?"

"Yep," he said. I watched him in the rearview mirror nod. "I'm good to go."

I shook my head. *I wonder will me and Bay be like them when we get old.*

I felt funny letting Mac, with his cane, pump the gas while I sat there and waited. Miss Vivee hummed some little ditty as she swiped face powder on her face with her red cosmetic sponge. Smug as a bug in the rug.

"All set," Mac said and fell into the backseat. "Took nearly fifty dollars to fill it up," he said. "Gas prices are so high nowadays."

"Actually, Mac," I said. "Compared to the last few years, gas is pretty cheap."

"Really?"

"What's all this talk about money?" Miss Vivee got into the conversation. "You don't seem to care too much about it, trying to make Bay buy you the Hope Diamond."

"I did not," I said and frowned. "Did he tell you that?"

"Didn't have to, I know how you are."

"What?" I said.

Both Bay and Miss Vivee seemed to have the wrong impression of me.

"And how did that little dinner of yours go last night?" Miss Vivee asked as I hit my blinkers to take the ramp to the highway. "I'm not noticing anything coming from that finger of yours blinding my eyes."

I changed the subject.

"Gavin Tanner came to the Maypop this morning."

"Did not," Miss Vivee said.

I pursed my lips and nodded. "Yes he did."

"Well good Lord, why didn't you come and get me?" she asked.

"What did he want?" Mac said from the backseat.

"He wanted to explain to me why he was stealing flowers from Lincoln Park."

"How did you know he was stealing flowers?" Miss Vivee asked.

"I saw him."

"When?"

I hit the highway, got over in the fast lane, and told Miss Vivee and Mac how'd I'd seen Gavin Tanner and the conversation I'd had with him over breakfast.

"So it's about the land," Miss Vivee said after I finished my spiel.

"What, Vivee?" Mac asked.

"The murder. Those two wanted the land at Lincoln Park. That's why they killed Jack Wagner."

"What about the other woman?" I said.

"What other woman?" Miss Vivee asked.

"The one Gavin Tanner alluded to."

"Probably nobody," she said. "I told you that boy is nervous, fidgeting all around. Probably seeing things."

"Land must be worth a lot of money," Mac speculated. "To make them kill him for it."

"Doesn't matter how much something's worth," Miss Vivee said. "If they want it bad enough, a person'll do anything to get it."

"That's true," he said.

"Well my money's on Gavin Tanner," I said.

Miss Vivee chuckled. "I thought you liked him."

"I did. But you were right," I said. "He fidgets all the time, and it seems like he keeps trying to steer us in another direction. One other than his. First Robert Bernard and Camren Wagner were in cahoots. Now there's this mysterious woman, and he's stealing flowers. And he doesn't know his father, maybe he found out it was Jack Wagner, he confronted him and Jack rejected him."

"What an imagination," Miss Vivee said.

Me with the vivid imagination? I don't think so.

"It just seems fishy to me," I said. "And he got all excited when he told us about those fruit trees."

"Maybe so," Mac said. "But he had nothing to gain. Dead or alive he couldn't get those flowers without sneaking around. Jack Wagner wanted to protect them, and Robert Bernard, if you believe Gavin's story, wanted to dig them all up."

"I still don't like him," I said as we arrived at the Walmart on Wrightsboro.

Hand over hand, I wrenched the seemingly *non*-power-steering wheel around. I carefully maneuvered, at a snail's pace, Miss Vivee's 1994, light blue, Lincoln Boatmobile, I mean Town Car, into a handicap parking spot near the door at Walmart. I knew if I hit any late model vehicle, her steel framed car would crush it.

I climbed out the car, and wiped the sweat off the back of my thighs from the leather-like seat, and tugged on my sundress. I went around to the other side and dragged open the heavy passenger door.

Miss Vivee looked over her double glasses at me. "C'mon on," I said. "Let's get you fixed up with a new pair of sunglasses."

"Me and Mac'll wait here," she said.

I frowned at her. "You have to get them fitted," I said.

"Oh phooey," she said and waved me off. "I have a normal sized face. If you bought the right kind, they'll do just fine."

I shook my head and looked in the backseat at Mac. He just shrugged and stayed put.

"Fine," I said and shut the creaky, oversized door. I wasn't going to argue with her.

I guess she thinks prescription frames are one size fits all.

I walked back around the car. I couldn't leave them in the hot weather with all the windows up. "Fine," I mumbled again and got in, cranked up the car, and pressed each button to let all the windows down.

"Turn the air on," Miss Vivee said.

Without saying anything, I reached over and turned the AC on high, and hit the switch to let the windows back up.

"Leave them down," Miss Vivee said.

"You want the windows down, and the air on?" I asked.

"Yeah. The air bothers my sinuses."

I took in a breath and blew it out through my nose. "Okay," I said in a huff. I found no logic in that, but who knew how her brain worked? I pushed on the door and got out. Walking to the store, I looked back at them. They looked okay.

It'll be quicker without the two of them anyway, I thought. I picked up my pace. I didn't want to leave them alone too long.

I knew I hadn't been gone more than five minutes. I had been the only person in Walmart's optometry department, and Miss Vivee's sunglasses were ready when I gave my name at the counter. I swiped my credit card through the reader, grabbed the package that included a free eyeglass case, and was headed out the door before the greeter finished checking one customer's long receipt. I was happy to have finished up quickly.

But coming to the second set of glass doors of the exit, I came to a screeching halt, and my happiness quickly drizzled. There, pulled up to the door, sat Miss Vivee's Lincoln Town Car. The back door of the car opened, I guessed for me, and Mac, sitting shotgun, was waving for me to hurry and get in the car. I walked up to the car and could see Miss Vivee sitting behind the wheel, holding it tight, her hands at ten and two. She focused her eyes straight ahead.

"C'mon, let's go," she said loudly. "And hurry it up."

"What the hey?" I slammed the back door and marched around the car to the driver's side. "Why is the car parked here, Miss Vivee?" I put my hand on my hip. "And why are you in the driver's seat?"

"We saw that man come out of the store," Miss Vivee said looking out the window at me. "We're going to follow him."

"Follow him?" I said. "Follow who?" I had to stop myself from shouting

"Robert Bernard," the two of them said in unison.

"Who is going to follow him?" I leaned forward so I could look at Miss Vivee.

"We are," they spoke at the same time again.

"And I'm driving," Miss Vivee added.

I should have never left those keys in the car.

"You can't drive." I stood defiantly outside of the car. "And why do we need to follow him? You don't even know where he's going."

"He's a murder suspect," Miss Vivee said. "You're the one who told me what Gavin Tanner said."

"He may lead us to something important," Mac said leaning over so he could see me through the driver's side window.

"Get in!" Miss Vivee yelled at me. Her voice high and squeaky. She was holding on to the wheel and stomping her feet. "We're gonna lose him."

"We can follow him," I said slowly, trying to reason with her. "But I need to drive." I lowered my voice to make it seem more calm, but still with a little bass to show some authority. I wanted to let her know I meant business. "You need to move back over to the passenger seat." I reached for the door handle and she pressed the lock. I heard the *click*. "Miss Vivee," was all I got out before she dug into me.

"Get. In." She warned again, still at four decibels over her usual speaking level, looking out the side of her eyes at me. "And, don't try to tell me what to do, Missy. Get in or Mac and I will leave without you." She revved the motor.

I scrambled to get the back door open, and vaulted into the back seat. I knew she'd do it, and I just couldn't image what would happen if I let the two of them take off without me. I scooted over and leaned forward between the two seats. "Miss Vivee," I started. "You need to let me -"

"I think I may have lost him," Miss Vivee interrupted me, concern obvious in her voice.

"No, Vivee," Mac said and pointed out the windshield. "He's right over there. I saw him pull out and turn left. "Hurry and we'll be able to catch him."

"Hurry?" I said. That word put fear in my heart. I clambered into a corner of the back seat, and felt around for a seat belt. There wasn't one. I dug down in the crevices. Nothing.

Did they even make seatbelts for the backseat in 1994?

I held onto the armrest.

"Okay." Miss Vivee said and nodded confirming Mac's update. Then she jerked with unnecessary force the gear shift located on the side of the steering wheel, putting it in drive. She yanked it so hard I thought she might've pulled it out. Then she rammed down on the gas. Everyone lurched forward.

"Oh my goodness!" I yelled out and gripped the armrest tighter. "Miss Vivee, I don't think you can do this."

"Do what?" she said putting on the blinkers and turning down a row of cars.

"Drive! Do a car chase! Get us *anywhere* safely."

"What do you think I'm doing now?" she said as she stepped on the brakes with too much pressure, making us reel forward. Then she didn't lift her foot again until we had slowed down so much that we were practically inching through the lot.

"I can drive, Miss Vivee." I was almost pleading with her now.

"Both of us can't drive, and I'm driving now." Her nose high to see over the wheel, she seemed to concentrate hard on moving through the lot. There weren't many cars, and I started hyperventilating anticipating how she'd act when there were actually other cars on the road. Then once we finally got out the store's parking lot, my heart came to a momentary halt as she let the car crawl into traffic on Wrightsboro Road.

Oh crap!

I closed my eyes and prayed.

Horns honking, brakes screeching, Miss Vive spoke over all the commotion. "Do you see him, Mac?" she asked. The same question she had solicited from him at least a half dozen times in the last minute and a half.

And each time Mac leaned forward and scanned the road ahead for Robert Bernard. "Not yet," Mac patiently replied.

"You want my glasses?" She reached up to pull hers off. "So you can be sure to spot him."

"No!" I said. "Don't take them off!"

"I don't need them, Vivee," Mac assured her.

I didn't know how he could stay so calm.

"Miss Vivee," I couldn't keep my voice at a normal level. "Please keep your glasses. You need them to see," I said, fear eking out in every word.

I don't know why I thought her wearing her glasses would make a difference in her driving. She was terrible at it. Right now, I just wanted to put a chokehold on whoever renewed her driver's license. I took in a deep breath and tried to calm my nerves.

Other cars were passing us, blowing their horns. We were moving, as Miss Vivee would say, slower than molasses in January. I didn't know how we'd ever catch anyone. Plus, Miss Vivee had no sense of gage for the pedals. She'd hit the brake too hard and pitch us forward, or press down on the gas, and thrust us back in our seats. The whole time not driving over

20mph. I was getting motion sickness, and I knew I'd have whiplash before it was all over.

"There he is," Mac said and pointed to a Mars red Mercedes SLC Roadster convertible stopped at a traffic light. "Hurry Vivee, make the light, he's turning the corner."

"Oh no! Miss Vivee," I said. "You can't follow *that* car."

"My car can keep up with any car on the road," Miss Vivee said proudly.

Not with you driving it!

She hit the gas, and did a hard turn, turning so deeply that she barely missed running up on the curb. I slid to the other side of the car and hit it with a *thud!*

"You can keep up with it, Vivee." Mac smiled at her. "Good job."

Miss Vivee pressed on the gas, and at the same time took her eye off the road to smile at Mac.

"Watch it, Vivee!" Mac cautioned. She was barreling into the back of the car in front of us. She hit the brakes like she was stomping out a fire, and I let out a yelp.

"For cryin' out loud," Miss Vivee said and glanced in her rearview mirror at me. "If you don't stop all that ruckus back there, you're going to make me cause a wreck."

Lord give me strength.

Chapter Twenty-Two

I wanted to get on my knees and kiss the ground.

Robert Bernard had evidently arrived at his destination and parked his car in front of what appeared to be a government building, making Miss Vivee finally stop the car. We had probably gone no more than six or seven miles from the Walmart we had visited, although the ride seemed so much longer to me.

"Okay," Miss Vivee said opening the car door, the car still running.

"What are you doing, Miss Vivee?" I shrieked, my voice and legs shaky.

"I want you to park it," she said. "I'm not good at parallel parking."

No kidding.

"Well, you just can't stop in the middle of the street and get out." She was in one of the two driving lanes. I turned around and looked out the back window. Cars were started to pile up behind us.

"Well, you can't park it if I keep driving it," she said and stepped out of the car paying no never mind to me or the oncoming traffic. "C'mon, Mac. Let's see what this man is up to."

"Are you going to wait until I park the car?" I asked and climbed out the backseat.

"Do you want us to lose him after I followed him all the way here?" she said. "You know following behind that little red racing car of his was no easy feat."

You're telling me.

"I'd hate for all my hard work to go for naught," she added.

"Fine," I found myself saying again. "I'll park and you go and find your murder suspect. One, I might add, who has given you no reason to think he's done anything murderous."

"He's in my notebook. That's all the reason I need."

I rolled my eyes. He was only on her list because she wrote his name there. I didn't care what Gavin Tanner said, there was nothing making me think he had killed Jack Wagner. He'd have to be pretty bold to still come and see Widow Wagner if he had.

I eased behind the driver's seat, closed my eyes and took in a breath. I opened them and stared at the dashboard. I needed to figure some way to disable the car after today so what just happened would never happen again.

Maybe I could set it afire, I thought as I pulled off.

I circled around the block amid lots of traffic and lights, and tried to find a spot in the parking lot next to the building once I made it back around. Nothing available. So, I drove back out onto the street and pulled into a spot right in front of the building in almost the same spot where I'd dropped them off. Robert Bernard's red car was nowhere in sight and neither were Grandma Bonnie and Grandpa Clyde.

Oh crap.

It was probably karma that I was having such a wild day with Miss Vivee. I had insisted that she get those glasses when she couldn't have cared less about them.

I parked the car and got out. I needed to find where they'd gone. And knowing Miss Vivee, the quicker I found out where they were, the better for everyone concerned. As I walked briskly to the door, I figured they couldn't have gotten too far because driving or walking, they didn't move fast.

The brown brick building that I'd parked in front of was the John H. Ruffin, Jr. Courthouse. I passed under the massive ivory-colored columns and in through the glass doors.

Great. Right into the den of the law. I'd never have enough money to bail Miss Vivee out for all her criminal offenses.

When I got inside, and made it through the metal detector, Miss Vivee was standing on the other side, waving me to hurry in.

"What took you so long?" she asked pulling me in close.

"We're in the middle of downtown. It's a lot of traffic out there and no place to park."

"Phooey," she said. "I could have had it parked in a jiffy if I'd had my parking glasses."

Parking glasses?

"I had to send Mac to follow that Robert Bernard so we could see what he was up to because he would've recognized me," Miss Vivee continued. "I wish I had thought to bring a disguise."

How she thought she could masquerade as anything other than the five-foot-nothing, ninety-something, nosey Nelly that she was, was a mystery to me.

"Why do we even care what he's doing here, Miss Vivee?"

"Because he's up to something," she said.

"Yeah. Probably minding his own business," I said and sighed. "Where did they go?" I asked. "Because Robert Bernard's car isn't outside anymore. Mac didn't leave with him, did he?"

Miss Vivee clicked her teeth. "Of course not."

I had to ask because it was no telling with them what was going on.

"So where is Mac, then?" I turned around to look for him.

"He had to go to the little boy's room. He'll be right out."

I took in a breath. "So why are you hurrying me along?"

"Mac told me that when he followed Robert Bernard he saw him go into Probate Court."

Was that supposed to be an answer to my question?

"O-kaaay." I said, not sure if I should attach some significance to what she said. "And what did he do there?"

"I don't know," she said and flailed her arms. "Mac's bladder couldn't hold out long enough for him to tell me."

"Well there he is now." I pointed. "He can tell us."

"Mac!" Miss Vivee called as if he hadn't seen us. She motioned him to move a little quicker. He tried but his limp slowed him down. I shook my head. "What did you see," she whispered to him.

"He looked at a file."

"Do you know which one?" she asked.

"No, but he had to sign it out. I figured we could check the ledger."

"Oh my Lord," I said. "Are we really going to check on a file he looked at? What are the odds that it has to do with *anything* we know something about?"

"You can come with us, or you can wait in the car," Miss Vivee said. "But I'm going to look at that file."

"Let's go," I said.

When we got to the probate office there was a big opening in the far wall with a sign over it that said File Room. A counter was fitted in the opening, and behind it was a room filled with files, and sitting behind a desk, I guessed, the file attendant. He had thin dark brown hair and his face was round and flushed. His blue and gold stripped tie fit loosely around his neck, and he had flecks of the powdered donut he was eating all over it and his mouth.

"That's what he signed," Mac said and pointed to an 11x14 card stock sign-in sheet with lines on it filled with writing. It sat on the marble-like counter. I pulled it close to me and looked at it. Miss Vivee saddled up next to me, put on her glasses she'd been holding in her hand, and perused the sheet.

"If you want a file you have to sign it out," File Attendant guy told us in between bites of his donut.

"We want a file," Miss Vivee said, her voice exuding confidence, but I knew she didn't know what she was asking for.

The man stuffed the rest of his powdery pastry in his mouth, licked his fingers and then wiped them on a napkin. He got up from his seat and wobbled over to us, the waist of his navy dress pants under his ginormous stomach, and the button on his light blue shirt pulling apart.

Miss Vivee ran her finger down the list and stopped on "Robert Bernard." She pointed to his name and I followed with my finger across the sheet to the "Case No." column. He had checked out file 2016 EST 102546. Whatever that meant.

"We want this one," Miss Vivee said pushing my finger out the way.

"You have to sign for it," the File Attendant and I said at the same time.

I picked up the pen that had long silver chain hooked to one end and attached to the wall at the other. But before I could write, Miss Vivee leaned over to me and said, "Put Mac's name on there."

I looked at her questioningly. She frowned in response. "Well, I don't want anyone to know I did it," she said.

I shook my head and wrote "Dr. Macomber Whitson," on the ledger. It asked for the time, so I glanced up at the clock on the wall. 10:30.

Still early, I thought. *Plenty of time left for Miss Vivee to get us into some kind of trouble.*

I put the time down and copied the case number off the line with Robert Bernard's name. Once done, I pushed the clipboard toward the File Attendant who was waiting patiently by, still chewing on the mouthful he had stored in his cheek.

File Attendant guy turned the ledger around to face him and said, "102546." He looked at us. "Pretty popular file today."

"What do you mean?" Mac asked.

"I had two other people come in this morning to look at this file. One just left." He went over to his desk and pulled a brown folder from his wire mesh file holder. "I hadn't even had the chance to put it back yet."

"Do tell?" Miss Vivee said and reached for the folder.

"You can take it out if you need to make copies. Copy counter is down the hallway. It's ten cents a page. And they're tables over there," he pointed through an archway into a smaller room that annexed the one we were in. "If you need to sit down and read through it." He looked at Mac and Miss Vivee.

"Thank you," Miss Vivee said taking her glassed off, she smiled sweetly.

I knew it was all fake.

We went to the next room. It was small and had several long wooden with wood chairs placed around them. Mac and Miss Vivee picked a table and sat on one side of it and I went around to the other side. She held the folder in her lap and placed her purse on the table and started digging down it.

"I can't believe you didn't ask who the other person was that looked at the folder," I said to Miss Vivee. I pulled out a chair and sat in it.

"Didn't have to," she said. She took out her "Suspects" notebook, and her No. 2 pencil. She flipped open the pad, finding a clean sheet she starting writing across the page. "They had to sign it out," she said as she wrote. "So, I looked at the ledger. It was checked out at eight-thirty this morning by 'Heritage Consultants.'" She tucked her notebook back into her purse and put her glasses on. She picked up the folder. "Well, looka here." She smiled and slid the folder across the table to me.

The brown, innocuous folder marked 2016 EST 102546 was in fact, the file for the Estate of Jackson Wagner.

Chapter Twenty-Three

Filled with paperwork, that included a will, a motion to contest the will, and an application to administer the estate, the contents of the file folder that Robert Bernard has checked were nothing more to me, than a bunch of legalese. But the one thing we all understand was that Miss Vivee's suspicious land developer was interested in what Jack Wagner had left behind. And that's all Miss Vivee needed to know.

"See. I told you," she said with a big smile on her face. "He *is* up to something."

"Doesn't mean he killed him," I said.

"And it doesn't mean he didn't," Miss Vivee said she picked through the papers in the folder."And why is someone contesting the will?" She lifted the stapled pages from the folder and stared at it.

"I don't know," I said. "I guess they didn't like what was in it."

"Well of course they didn't, I know that. But what didn't they like?" Miss Vivee said as she flipped through the pages and then pushed it over to me. "Here. Tell me what it says."

I stared at it too. I didn't know what all that stuff meant.

"We'd need a lawyer to understand what's in this folder," Mac offered. "Lawyer speak always looks a lot of mumble jumbo to people who aren't trained in the field."

"Oh phooey," Miss Vivee said. "It couldn't be that hard to understand." She gave me the rest of the pile of papers from the file. "See if you can make heads or tails of it."

I whipped out my phone. "No need to," I said. "My uncle and my brother are lawyers. I'm going to email my brother, Micah, and attach copies."

"He'll be able to understand it?" Miss Vivee asked.

I didn't bother to answer. If he couldn't my parents would be very upset with all the money they dished out for that law degree of his. I started taking pictures with the camera on my phone and sending them to Micah.

"Okay," I said, clicking send on the last email. "He should get back with me in a bit." I put my phone in my pocket. "So what now?" I asked. "We ready to head back to Yasamee?

"No," Miss Vivee said, and it looked to me like she rolled her eyes. "We go and visit Heritage Consultants."

"What? Why?" I asked.

I could feel lies and trouble a-brewing.

"To see what their connection is to Jack Wagner."

"And how do you plan on doing that?" I asked, although I was sure I'd regret the answer.

She racked the file folders contents back towards her, hit the ends of them on the table and put them neatly back inside. "We have to follow the clues."

"Okay." I stood up. No use in arguing. I'd go along, and brace myself for the worse. But what I wanted to tell her was that the only clue I knew we had for sure was the one recited in the note. But, I also knew she'd all but dismissed that poem after she decided none of the flowers in it had killed Jack Wagner, even if the flower names did spell the murder weapon.

I looked at the two of them. "Let's go." I reached across the table and picked up the folder. I headed back over to the File Room counter to return it, and spoke to them over my shoulder. "And I'm driving," I said.

ƐƷƐƷƐƷƐƷƐƷƐƷƐƷƐƷ

We piled back in the car and sat with the air on outside of the courthouse while I Googled Heritage Consultants. Miss Vivee made me read out loud everything I found. And what I found was unbelievable – at least to me. I discovered that Heritage Consultants was owned by a Debra and Lance Goodall. I clicked on the link that the search engine had provided and a great big ole grin came across my face as I read their home page.

Heritage Consultants were an archaeological firm.

I felt like Miss Vivee with the flowers at Krieger Gardens. Happy. It was like Marigold had said, you don't meet an archaeologist just anywhere. But now we were going to visit two of them.

I read the "About" section on their website out loud to Miss Vivee and Mac. It said that they provided archaeological impact evaluations, historical research, preservation and structure surveys, and cultural resources investigations for real estate development, and government agencies in the southern United States, such as those that work under the National Historic Preservation Act.

I couldn't wait to talk to them.

Their office was located not too far from where we had started out at Walmart. I clicked on directions and did a U-turn – not the best decision on a busy street, but certainly not as reckless as Miss Vivee's driving.

I got out of the downtown area and headed back down Wrightsboro Road. I had flashbacks of Miss Vivee driving down it the entire time we were on it, and exhaled a sigh of relief when I turned off onto Walton Way. Their office, 2122 Central Avenue, was a small brick storefront, attached to a larger one that had a huge yellow sign across the top, with red writing that read, "Going Out of Business Sale." The stones on the front of their side of the building had been painted white a long time ago, and were now dingy with chipping paint.

Definitely not what I had expected.

There were diagonal parking slots out front, and I found a spot without any problem. I helped Miss Vivee out of the car, and the three of us went up to the door.

"Heritage Consultants" was painted in white on the glass door, which was flanked on either side by two huge picture windows. A little bell tinkled as we opened the door and went into a small office. There were a couple of chairs, an older green couch, and a desk that was cluttered with papers and folders. A shelf sat behind it with maps, 3-ring binders, a printer, and office supplies. And there was no one in sight.

Didn't they hear the bell?

Whenever we were on one of Miss Vivee's fact-finding excursions, I usually stepped back and waited for her to do her thing. I didn't talk, unless she asked me a direct question because I never knew what outrageous story she'd come up with to get the answers she needed. But this time, I thought I'd take the lead.

"We'll be right with you," a voice finally came from a back area.

"Okay," I answered back.

"Let me do the talking," Miss Vivee said.

"It's an archaeological firm, Miss Vivee. I know the lingo."

"Lingo, smingo," Miss Vivee said. "I've got this." She winked at me and made a clicking sound with her mouth. "You just hang back."

Hang back?

205

"Fine," I said and went and leaned on the wall – arms folded across my chest, one leg crossed over the other – next to the desk. I let my eyes wander around the room. It was a mess, papers everywhere, but the pictures, old style black and white ones that were hung on the walls, did interest me. I pushed off and started to take a look at them when a blue folder on the desk caught my eye. It had a label on it with a long number and "Lincoln Park" written in large black letters.

Oh my goodness!

"Miss Vivee!" She and Mac had sat on the worn, rust-colored seat cushions of the metal chairs that were in front of the desk. "Look!" I pointed to the folder. "That's why they were checking on the probate file, to find out about the land." I said in a strained whisper.

Miss Vivee stood up and leaned over the desk. "What's in it?" she whispered back, her eyes wide in anticipation.

I hunched my shoulders. "I don't know," I said.

"Get it!" Miss Vivee's whisper crackled with excitement.

"What?"

"Get that folder," she said a little louder and pointed to it.

"Shhh!" I said. I had heard her, I just couldn't believe what she wanted me to do. Then, before I could answer her, she snatched the folder off the desk, fell back into her seat and stuffed it down into her purse.

Oh Lord!

"Hello," a woman came out the back just as Miss Vivee snapped her purse shut. "I'm Debra Goodall."

Not one of us said a word. I didn't speak because I was in shock and, luckily, had been instructed not to. I didn't know what was wrong with Miss Vivee, but one thing for sure, I knew that little ninety-something heart of hers was racing.

Debra Goodall wore her fine brown hair long and straight, parted on the side, she had a habit of sweeping it behind her ear, even when it was already there. She had narrow brown eyes that she accentuated with black eyeliner, and a light application of blue eye shadow. She was about 5'6" with a shapely build. But I didn't think it was from exercising because she inhaled often when she spoke, as if she couldn't get in enough air at one time to voice an entire sentence.

She looked at the three of us expectantly. "May I help ya'll?"

"I need the little girl's room," Miss Vivee said and stood up.

"We don't have a public restroom," she said looking confused. "You can go to the gas station down the street."

"She's an archaeologist," Miss Vivee said. She sat back down and pointed at me. "She needs to talk to you, but really," she started shaking her leg and pushing down in her seat, "I have to go to the restroom. It's really not good for you to deny a woman of my age the use of your facilities. It could get quite messy."

Debra Goodall looked at me, then at Miss Vivee. "It's right down that hallway," she pointed. "First door on the left, right past the table with the coffee maker on it."

"Thank you," Miss Vivee said. "C'mon, Mac."

Consultant Goodall looked at Miss Vivee. "Are you taking him with you?"

"We do everything together," Miss Vivee said. "Have been for the last fifty years."

Mac got up and followed Miss Vivee down the hall.

"Are they okay?" Debra Goodall asked. "I mean . . . Is something wrong with the two of them?"

I laughed. "I don't think it would be too far off or impolite to say that they are a little weird."

Debra laughed with me, then pointed to a seat. "Have a seat."

"Actually," I said. "I wanted to take a closer look at the pictures on the walls. These are excavations you've done?" I asked and walked over to a picture on the opposite wall.

I had to come up with something fast, I didn't know what Miss Vivee was up to with that folder and Mac in the restroom. But I figured I'd better keep Archeologist Goodall busy.

"Yes," she said proudly. "But that was years ago. We don't go out on digs anymore. What about you?" She looked at me. "I don't meet an archaeologist every day."

"I know, right?" I said and smiled. "But I am. So is my mother. She's a Biblical archaeologist and used to take us kids out on digs with her. I caught the bug."

"Wow," Debra said. "That's cool."

"Is this your husband?" I pointed to a man in one of the pictures with her.

"Yes. That's Lance." She came stood next to me. "Although we weren't married yet when that was taken."

"Is he an archaeologist, too?"

"No. He's a geologist. He's the reason that I stopped going out on digs, and started this little firm."

"You miss it?" I asked. "Excavating?"

She stared at the picture, looking at it thoughtfully, and didn't say anything for a long minute. "Sometimes I do," she said and looked at me, a half smile on her face. She took in a breath. "What about you? You've been out on any digs lately?"

"Yeah," I said. "Over at Stallings Island."

"Get out of here! That was you? You're the one who found the extinct – well thought to be extinct fish?"

I smiled. She had heard about me. "Yep. That was me."

"Oh. My. God. Lucky you!" She said. "Congrats. I read all about it in my subscription of Archaeology."

She patted me on my back. "It's nice to have you in my humble little office."

"We're back," Miss Vivee announced as she and Mac came through the doorway.

"Are you okay?" I asked and raised an eyebrow.

"We're fine, Dear," Miss Vivee said.

"Do you need to sit down," Debra asked. She nodded to the chairs and the two went and sat down.

"That coffee smells so delicious." Miss Vivee blew out a breath like she was winded from running a marathon. "Could I get a cup?" Miss Vivee asked.

"It may be a little stale," Debra said. "I had made it earlier this morning."

"Just like I like it," Miss Vivee said. "Hours old." She smiled at Debra.

"Would you like a cup, too?" Debra Goodall asked Mac.

"No, he doesn't want any," Miss Vivee said.

"Okay," Debra said and looked at me. Before she asked if I wanted some of the old brew, I shook my head "no."

She headed down the hallway, and as soon as she disappeared, Miss Vivee whipped that crumbled folder out of her purse and threw it across the desk.

"You can't leave that there like that," I went back to speaking in a strained whisper. "Look at it!"

Miss Vivee stood straight up and glared at me, not saying a word.

"You don't think she'll notice that?" I pointed to the bent up blue folder sitting on top of all the clutter on the desk, standing out like a sore thumb.

"Do you take cream and sugar?" Debra yelled from the back.

"Yes," Miss Vivee yelled back. "Two creams, and seven sugars."

"Seven?" came the response. "You want seven teaspoons of sugar?"

It seemed her voice was getting closer. I went to the doorway, and met her just as she was getting back to office area. I stood in front of her. "Yes. Seven teaspoons." I said.

"It's just a little cup," Debra Goodall said and waved the small, white Styrofoam cup at me.

"Seven." I nodded my head vigorously. "Is that alright?" I asked.

"Sure," she said. "Hope she brought her insulin," she mumbled as she headed back down the hall. "She'll probably have to drink it straight from the bottle."

I turned to see Miss Vivee sticking that rumpled folder under some paper on the desk.

"Miss Vivee!"

"What?" she said and snatched her hand back. Then she narrowed her eyes at me. "Don't yell at me, Missy."

"I didn't yell, Miss Vivee," I said whispering. I started opening drawers. "I'm just a little anxious."

"What are you doing?" she said.

"Looking for another blue folder."

"For what?" she asked.

I stopped what I was doing, and tilted my head. I looked at her quizzically.

"What?" she asked.

"Because you broke that one," I said and pointed to the one partially hidden on the desk. "We need to fix it."

"You can't actually *break* a folder," Mac said. His first words since we'd been there. "It's made out of stock paper. She just bent it up a little."

"A little?" I said. "Mac, please!" I turned to look on the shelf behind the desk.

Did he really think he needed to explain to me the make-up of a folder? Geesh!

"Bingo!" I said as I came upon a box of multi-colored folders. I grabbed a blue one, and turned back to the desk, fishing out the Lincoln Park folder from where Miss Vivee had tried to hide it.

"How do you think you're going to transfer that label to the new folder?" Miss Vivee asked.

"Oh crap," I said.

"Dearie!" Miss Vivee yelled out. "Yoohoo! Debra Goodall!"

"What are you doing?" I said a little louder than I meant to. I turned to see if Debra was coming, and at the same time tried to stick the folders behind my back.

"Here, I come," Debra said.

"No!" Miss Vivee said. "Don't come. I just wanted to tell you that Mac wanted a cup of coffee. Could you bring him one?"

"What?" she said. She had come back down the hall anyway and was standing in the doorway, one cup of coffee in her hand. I had backed up against the wall, both folders behind my back.

Miss Vivee smiled a seven-spoons-of-sugar-smile at her. "Mac would like a cup, too."

Debra Goodall looked at Mac, and he smiled at her. "I thought he didn't want any coffee."

"He changed his mind," Miss Vivee said.

Debra looked at him, then at me. "Does he talk?" she asked.

"Of course he does," Miss Vivee said. "How else would I have known he wanted coffee?" She furrowed her brow and shook her head.

Debra took in a breath, turned on her heels with the one cup still in her hand.

I pulled the folders from behind my back as soon as Debra Goodall disappeared. Laying the new folder on the desk, I tried to pull off the label. It wouldn't budge. I looked at Miss Vivee and Mac. They looked back at me.

"Crap."

Then I remembered I'd seen a pair of scissors in the middle desk drawer. I retrieved them and cut the tab with the label attached off. Then I cut the tab off the new folder and pulled a piece of tape off the dispenser that sat on the desk.

"*Voila!*" I waved the folder in the air. They wouldn't realize anything was amiss until they handled the folder, hopefully by then, we'd be long gone. Then I removed the contents from the original folder and pressed them flat as best I could and placed them inside the file. I tried to put the folder back in the same spot Miss Vivee had confiscated it from. I folded the crinkled folder and gave it to Miss Vivee. "Here," I said. "Put this in your purse."

Miss Vivee clicked her purse shut just as I heard Debra Goodall come back in. She had a cup of coffee in each hand.

"I put seven sugars in his, too," she said. "You two seem to be one, so I figured that would be just about right."

They took the cups and each took a sip. "Mmmm," they said in unison.

"Where's Lance?" Miss Vivee asked. She was muscling her way back in the conversation after not having a substantive word to say, and acting looney for most of our visit.

"Lance?" Debra Goodall asked.

"Yes. Isn't that your husband's name?"

"Yes, it is." Debra looked surprised that Miss Vivee knew that.

"Is he here?" she asked

Debra Goodall looked at me with a smirk then back at Miss Vivee. "As a matter of fact, he came in when I was making the coffee. He's in the back."

"Well my husband and I have a thousand acres of land in the Black Belt down in Freemont County."

There she goes with that lie again.

"In the Black Belt?" That seemed to pique Debra's interest. She threw back her shoulders and glanced back through the doorway down the hall.

"What are you doing with your land?" Debra asked looking back at Miss Vivee.

"Having it surveyed for its historical significance."

"Are you serious?" she asked.

"As a heart attack," Miss Vivee said locking eyes with her.

"I'll get my husband," she said.

Lance Goodall was tall and lanky. He looked to be in his early thirties, and had a light five o'clock shadow with red undertones, the same color as the highlights peppered throughout his head of thick, light brown hair. He had on skinny leg jeans, a plaid shirt, and beige tie and suit jacket that all looked outdated and too small.

He got right into the conversation as he came into the room.

"How did you get that land?" he asked Miss Vivee.

"Hello," she said. "You're Lance Goodall."

"Oh yes," Debra spoke up. "This is my better half," she smiled at Mac. "Lance this is-" she stopped. "You know, I don't think I ever got your names."

"I'm Vivienne Caspard-Whitson."

"And I'm Dr. Macomber Whitson," Mac said and smiled. "Vivienne's my better half."

"Ahh, you do speak," Debra said.

"So back to my question," Lance said.

"It has been in my family for generations," Miss Vivee picked back up with her lie without batting an eye. "I have the family version of how it was acquired, but I'd like to know for sure."

"So you came to us?" he asked.

"Isn't that what you do?" Miss Vivee asked.

"Yes, it is."

"And I heard you did the historical preservation survey on Lincoln Park."

The Goodalls looked at each other.

"Who told you that?" Lance asked.

"We're involved in several social circles," Mac said.

"We heard that you're the ones that get the important jobs like that," Miss Vivee said. "So we decided to come and see you."

"To help us out with our land." Mac patted his pocket. "We brought our checkbook."

The Goodalls looked at each other again, this time they smiled.

"So tell us about that project," Mac said. "The one you did at Lincoln Park."

"Well," Lance cleared his throat and seemed to think about what to say. He started out speaking slowly. "We were hired by the City of Augusta," he said. "That's how we get our contracts, through various political subdivisions, such as municipalities."

"Well we get most of them that way," Debra said.

"Right," Lance said.

"About ninety-five percent of the time," Debra said. "Then there's private owners, like yourselves, that hire us."

"Right. We conduct surveys of lands in certain districts that are believed should be included in the National Register of Historic Places."

"Just like your land," Debra said. "They're recommended based on stories passed down from generation to generation about the history of the land."

"Was it one?" Miss Vivee asked.

"Was what one?" Debra asked.

"Lincoln Park. Was it in an historical district?"

"No," Debra said.

"We don't think so," Lance added. "We were hired to supplement the information on the area surrounding it that had been listed in the National Register around thirty-five years ago. We just turned in our report, so it still has to be decided on."

"Right," Debra said. "But we needed to collect more data on the developmental history of the neighborhood. So there's still that to do." She swallowed, taking in a breath and looked at Lance.

"Attempting to amend the historic district boundaries can be tedious." Lance Goodall took over her explanation.

They spoke in tandem, like they were like a tag-team wrestlers. And like it was rehearsed.

"And what exactly did you find out?" Miss Vivee asked.

I saw Debra Goodall's eyes go from that blue folder on that desk to her husband and then down to her hands. She didn't say a word.

"Why would you be interested in that?" Lance Goodall asked.

"At our age, we tend to be interested in everything. Nothing much else left for us to do," Miss Vivee smiled one of her fake smiles, "but count our money and ask questions."

Mac patted the pocket where he claimed the checkbook was again.

"So what did you find out?" Miss Vivee asked.

"As I said, we submitted what we had, and then we still have to do supplemental work before it's all finished," Lance answered, his wife's words seemed to have left her.

"Well, my good man, I'm convinced," Mac said. He stood up and stuck out his hand.

Lance took his hand and shook it. "Convinced? About what?"

"You are the people to take care of our land. You two seem to know what you're talking about and are in sync with each other and I like that. Don't you like that, Vivee?"

"Mmm hmm." Miss Vivee nodded her head.

"So what we'll do," Mac said, "is have our granddaughter drive us to our safe deposit box."

"This is your granddaughter?" Lance asked.

"Oh honey," Debra said. "I forgot to introduce you, this is Logan Dickerson. She's an archaeologist."

"How did you know her name?" Miss Vivee said.

"I read about her work on Stallings Island. I'm sure y'all are very proud of her."

Evidently not proud enough of me to leave me their imaginary land in the Black Belt.

"We are, Mac said. "Now. We'll get our copy of our property papers, old surveys, plat numbers and the like, and bring them all to you."

"Okay," Lance said. He looked at his wife, both seemed surprised at the turn of events.

"It's a big project, Lance," Mac said. "And an expensive one, I'm sure. But we're prepared." Mac patted his pocket again. "And we'll need it done quickly because as you can see, we don't know how much longer we'll have."

"We understand, and we'll keep that in mind," Debra answered.

Chapter Twenty-Four

"Have you ever met bigger liars in all your life?" Miss Vivee said. She pulled out her new pair of sunglasses and put them on.

Yep. I thought. *I'm sitting in the car with them.*

We had left Heritage Consultants without incident, in fact all had been quite pleasant taking into account Miss Vivee's acts of thievery. But Miss Vivee's sickly sweet smile evaporated as soon as we stepped out into the sunlight. And then she got started on them as soon as she got settled into the car. She pulled out her notebook, found a pencil, licked the tip of it and started scrawling.

"I swear," Miss Vivee continued her rant once she put the notebook up. "I have half a mind to call Bay right now and have him and Sheriff Haynes come and arrest those two."

"For what?" I asked.

"Murder!"

Oh Lord.

"Don't you roll your eyes at me, Missy" she said and smacked my arm. "Those two are guilty as sin."

"What did they do?"

"Are you deaf? I told you, they murdered Jack Wagner."

"Why?" I asked.

"Why what?" she asked.

"Why do you think they killed Jack Wagner?" I said.

"Because they had stolen his money, and he had threatened to sue them. They would have lost their business, their livelihood and their reputation. So they put a stop to him telling anything to anybody. Permanently."

"Why do you say that? Is that what was in that file?" I asked.

"That they killed him?" she said. "Why would they put that there?"

"No, Miss Vivee." I changed my question around. "What was in the file?"

"Jack Wagner had hired Heritage Consultants to find out the history of his land," Mac said from the backseat.

"Why?" I asked.

"Is that all you can say?" Miss Vivee scrunched up her face and poked out her lip. "Why, why, why." She swung her head from side to side. "Who knows why," she said. "All I know is that they did it."

"I think that he'd found out that the land adjacent to his had been included in the historical registry," Mac offered. "He wanted to see if his land had any historical value."

221

I wanted so bad to ask 'why' but I looked at Miss Vivee and decided against it.

"So . . ." I started. I wanted to frame my question correctly. "I take it that the Goodalls took payment for the work, but didn't complete it."

"See what happens when you use that noggin of yours?" Miss Vivee said.

I still didn't have enough information to come to the conclusion that they had murdered Jack Wagner. Evidently, Miss Vivee did.

"If you cheat, you'll lie, and if you lie, you'll steal," Miss Vivee was still venting.

"What did they steal?" I asked.

"Jack Wagner's life!"

"So, I take it, Miss Vivee, that you don't like the Goodalls?"

"There is nothing *good* about those people."

"I just wish someone would tell me what was in that file that's got you so worked up," I said.

"Well, from what I understood from the file, in the little time we had it," Mac said. "It appeared that the State of Georgia passed out federal grants to conduct historic preservation projects. They skipped over the land where Lincoln Park is located. So Mr. Wagner paid Heritage Consultants to do it. Survey it and find out if it should be listed in the registry.

"I'm thinking that the state then reconsidered and gave them money to do the study on that plot of land as well. The Goodalls neglected to let Mr. Wagner know they got grant money, or that they'd been hired by the state after he'd hired them."

"What made the registry reconsider?"

"Not sure," Mac said. "Maybe it was just an oversight on its part in the first place."

"All this was in that file?" I asked. I hadn't noticed much in there.

"There were two letters that told the story," Mac said. "One from the state, the other from a very upset Jack Wagner."

"But wh-" I started.

"Don't you say 'why,'" Miss Vivee warned.

"The Goodalls told us that there wasn't any historical value to the property," I said instead.

"They lied," Miss Vivee said.

"How do you know that?" I asked.

"If all the land surrounding a piece of land is historical, you think one chunk of it sitting smack dab in the middle isn't?" Miss Vivee shook her head. "Whatever made the other land special just hopped right over it, and continued its historical purpose on the other side?"

I guess that made sense.

"Is that the way you do your digs?" Miss Vivee kept going. "You find something in the dirt in one place, skip over the next acre or two then start digging again there?"

"Okay, Miss Vivee," I said and threw up my hands. "I get it."

"Well get it with your hands on the wheel." She looked over at me. "Please."

"Was there some kind of report in that folder?" I asked. I put both hands on the wheel, flicked on the blinkers, and switched lanes. "A report from their survey?"

"I told you that they didn't do anything," Miss Vivee said.

"No," Mac said. "We didn't see any kind of report."

"What about means and opportunity, Miss Vivee?" I looked over at her. "They weren't even at the fair."

"You didn't *see* them at the fair. There's a difference," she said. "And then there was that framed blue ribbon hanging on the wall. Didn't you see it?"

"No," I said. I'd only seen pictures of excavation sites. "A blue ribbon for what?"

"Baking competition. Awarded to Lance Goodall."

"What does that mean?"

"He knows how to bake is what it means. That's opportunity," Miss Vivee said. "And as for the means, you said anybody could buy bitter almonds in South America. From the Amazon."

"From the Amazon?" I said confused.

"Yeah, you read it off your phone."

"Oh," I said understanding. "*On* Amazon."

"Right," Miss Vivee said hesitating at the way I said it. "In South America," she emphasized. "Wouldn't take but a couple of weeks to get here."

I didn't bother explaining the difference to her, but she was right, you could order them and have them mailed right to your doorstep. The dosage recommended to use to "cure" cancer wasn't lethal, but certainly if someone wanted a person dead, it wouldn't be hard to give him or her more than what was suggested as safe.

Miss Vivee seemed convinced about those two. But I knew she wasn't being logical about it. For some reason she just didn't like Debra and Lance Goodall, and that had been all it took for them to make it on her list of possible suspects. I may not have known her real reason, but I couldn't imagine it was because they were liars.

That would be pretty hypocritical of her.

I tried to connect the poem and flowers with the Goodalls and I couldn't do it. Debra Goodall, like me, liked to play in the dirt, but she probably didn't know what grew in it. And she seemed nice. Plus, she was an archaeologist. We don't murder people. But Lance . . . I wasn't so sure about him. Did a geologist know that the kernel of some fruits contained a substance that our bodies could convert to a poison? That would be a big stretch – knowing the physical properties of the earth to knowing what the fruit bore that grew in that earth. Still, he did seem deceitful and overbearing. Could he have convinced his wife to do something as bad as murder?

I couldn't find a reference in the poem to them, nor could I figure out how or why (dare I say that word) they would have done it.

Nope. I decided it wasn't them. Couldn't be. My money was still on Gavin Tanner.

"Whoa!" Miss Vivee let out a yelp, startling me out of my thoughts. "Did you see that?"

"Miss Vivee you can't scare me like that when I'm driving."

"You scared me when I was behind the wheel," Miss Vivee said. "Now you see how it feels."

"What did you see, Vivee?" Mac said.

"That was Robert Bernard in that car that just past. He had the top down now, but I know that car."

"We're not following him, Miss Vivee," I cautioned.

"Did you see who was in the car with him?" she asked. "The blonde woman?"

"I didn't see the car," I said.

"Who was it, Vivee?" Mac asked.

"Couldn't've been," Miss Vivee shook her head. "It couldn't have been her." She looked over at me. "I think it must be these new glasses you got me. They've got me seeing things." She pulled them off and looked at them before dumping them in her purse. Then she pulled out her prescription glasses and popped her old pair of sunglasses on top. "There," she said. "That's better."

Chapter Twenty-Five

Evidently, Miss Vivee wasn't completely convinced that the Goodalls were the culprits in Jack Wagner's death, because after we got home she asked me to take her to speak with Robert Bernard the next day. She looked troubled, like she had been trying to work out something in her head. And by wanting to see him, it appeared to me, she was still looking for the murderer. Why else, I thought, would she want to talk to Freckle Face?

After the house got quiet that night, I stretched across my bed, fired up my laptop and pulled up the Georgia Department of Natural Resources website. The tabs across the top indicated that there was an Archaeological page. I was tempted to click on it, but knew it would be just a distraction, so I moved the cursor over to the Historic Preservation Division page and opened it up.

Clicking through the pages I found that there were certain criteria and a nomination process for determining if a property should be registered. I found that to be considered "historic," a property must have three essential attributes: sufficient age, a relatively high degree of physical integrity, and historical significance.

The land at Lincoln Park was intact, well kept, and as land goes, I'm sure it was old. I didn't know of any historical significance to it. All I knew is that there had been a murder there more than a half century ago.

I learned a lot about the process reading the different pages offered on the site. Eventually I found a press release section. Among other news, it reported about ten Georgia cities that had received federal sub-grants from the Historic Preservation Fund to finance projects.

I wonder was that the one that included Jack Wagner's land?

I rolled over onto my back and stared at the ceiling. Miss Vivee was right. Everything we'd found out so far pointed to that land. Robert Bernard couldn't have been checking on anything but Jack Wagner's land at probate court. The Goodalls were supposed to have surveyed the land. Gavin Tanner was pulling up "expensive and exotic flowers" from an open field. A field that included lilies of the valley, which according to the poem were the most "grande." And it was Jack Wagner's land.

But which one of them were desperate enough for the land to kill Jack Wagner? Which one of them couldn't spell? And what the heck did that note have to do with any of it? The only person, or I guess I should say people, that the note tied to the murder were Camren Wagner, Gavin Tanner, and Miss Vivee.

I rolled back over on my stomach and propped my head up on a pillow. I just didn't see how anyone was going to figure this one out.

I pushed my laptop aside and drifted off to sleep. That night I dreamt of little people with blue faces skipping through a huge field picking flowers that bloomed cherry pies.

ɛɜɛɜɛɜɛɜɛɜɛɜɛɜɛɜ

We left early the next afternoon to go and find Robert Bernard. Miss Vivee came out the house with a dark tan-colored, leather blueprint tube that was almost as big as she was. I grabbed it, and we headed out. We took my jeep. When I announced I wasn't driving her big ole car anywhere, I didn't get one word from her. Perhaps she had given herself a fright as well. We swung by and picked up Mac, and for the third time in as many days, I drove up to Augusta.

Mr. Bernard did have an office, one listed on the Internet, and a pretty fancy one to boot. It was located in one of Augusta's historical districts, but unlike the Goodalls, he had a secretary who didn't let us get anywhere near any files.

Perhaps that was a good thing . . .

"Don't I know you?" he said after we got into his office. Mac and Miss Vivee sat down, she took her blue print tube from me, and I assumed my usual position holding up the wall.

"We represent the Historical Society of Freemont and Augusta Counties," Miss Vivee said.

"I do know you!" He snapped his fingers and pointed at me, then to Miss Vivee. "I thought that you owned a thousand acres of land that you wanted to donate?"

First time Miss Vivee ever got caught in one of her lies.

How was she going to get out of this one?

"That doesn't mean I'm not in the historical society," Miss Vivee said without missing a beat. "In fact, since I own more land than anyone else, they made me the president."

Man, she's good.

"A position she's held for the past fifty years," Mac added.

"Sugar," Miss Vivee said. "Not the last fifty years," she tapped his hand. "You'll have the man thinking I'm old."

Robert Bernard coughed.

We all looked at him. "Excuse me," he said. Something got caught in my throat." He flicked his power-red necktie. "So, what can I do for you? You want to talk to me about that land you own in the Black Belt?"

"Who is that woman in the pictures?" Miss Vivee pointed to family pictures sitting on the credenza behind him.

He turned around to look, then turned back to Miss Vivee.

"Why?" he asked.

"Is she your wife?"

"No. Well yes. We're separated."

"Didn't know you liked blondes."

"You don't know anything about me," he said, a small grin on his face. "So you were telling me about your land."

"No we weren't," Mac said.

"We're here about Lincoln Park," Miss Vivee said.

Well no beating around the bush on that one.

"Lincoln Park? What about it?" he asked.

"We want to know why you're building condos there."

"What?" he said, his face knitted in confusion.

"Camren Wagner told us that you were bulldozing that land to build condominiums."

No she didn't. I thought. *That was Gavin Tanner.*

"Do you think that that's the best use for the land?" Miss Vivee asked, a smirk on her face.

"I'm not building anything on that land," he said. "At least not at the moment."

"What does that mean? At the moment?" Miss Vivee narrowed her eyes.

"It means that as it stands right now, I'm not building condos."

"Did you find what you were looking for in Jack Wagner's probate file?" Miss Vivee asked.

Robert Bernard lifted an eyebrow, then it suddenly hit him what she was asking. "How do you know that I looked at that file?" he said. He slammed his hand on the desk and glared at the two of them, his eyes narrowed. He stood up as if he was signaling the end to the conversation.

"You seem upset, young man," Mac said.

"Sit down," Miss Vivee said. "We're just trying to find the best use for our land. Want to make sure you're trustworthy enough. That's a mighty big area we've got." Miss Vivee patted her blue print tube.

"We don't mean any harm by our questions," Mac said. "Might come out lucrative for you."

They were as good a tag-team as the Goodalls.

Robert Bernard seemed reluctant, but he did sit back down. "It's just that I could have made a lot of money off that deal. Lincoln Park is ripe for the picking." He shook his head.

"Best laid plans . . ." Mac said.

"Believe me, it wasn't because of a lack of trying."

"Did getting that land include wooing his wife?" Miss Vivee asked.

Robert Bernard lifted an eyebrow, then let a sly smile creep up his face. "Now you're doing too much," he said. "But that little dalliance, if you want to call it that, had nothing to do with that land. Camren's a beautiful woman – and an appealing one – in her own right. But, she'd never would have agreed to help me to convince him to let me build a condominium complex there. She loved it just as much as her husband did. But for different reasons."

"What was his reason for not building?" Mac asked.

"Who knows," Robert Bernard said and shook his head.

"What was her reason?" Miss Vivee asked.

"She wants to do a little developing of her own."

Abby L. Vandiver

Chapter Twenty-Six

We left Robert Bernard's office, none the wiser. At least in my opinion. Miss Vivee's questions hadn't seemed directed to finding out anything, and I hadn't the faintest idea why she cared about the blonde woman in the picture with him, unless it was the blonde she'd thought she saw in his car the day before. Once we got back in the car my phone rang. It was my brother, Micah.

"Hey, big brother."

As soon as I said his name, Miss Vivee started hitting me on my arm. "Make it so I can hear," she said.

"Hold on, Micah," I said. "I'm going to put you on speaker." I hit the icon. "Okay. Go ahead."

"Well your images didn't come over too clearly," he said, "but what I could make of it was that Jackson Wagner had set up a pour over will-"

"A what?" Miss Vivee yelled into the phone.

"He can hear you, Miss Vivee. You don't have to yell."

"Well, I can hardly hear him," she said in a normal voice. "Can you hear me?" She leaned in and yelled.

"Yes ma'am," Micah said. "I can hear you just fine. So a pour over will is one where the decedent's – uhm, the dead person's – assets are poured from the will into a trust so that those assets won't go through probate."

"Why would someone do that? Make a pour over will." I asked.

"Probate is costly and time consuming. Sometimes people don't want to make grieving loved ones go through the process. It's a lot of tedious paperwork. And one reason, the reason I'm guessing here is that trusts are not public record, so no one will know who is getting what. That way no one can contest it."

"But someone is contesting it, right?" I said. "Didn't I email you a copy of that?"

"You did, and someone is contesting it, but it probably won't hold up in court."

"Why not?"

"Well, you can only contest a trust for certain reasons, like fraud, or incompetence at the time it was drafted. But from what I gathered the pour-over will was just a safeguard in case anything else was later added. There appears to have been a living trust set up a long time ago. It leaves some land, uhm, let me see . . . Oh here it is, Lincoln Park to someone."

"Who?" Miss Vivee and Mac asked in unison.

"I'd have to see the trust papers to know that," he said. "But remember, trusts aren't public record, so it'd be nearly impossible for you to see those."

Please don't put any ideas in Miss Vivee's head.

I could hear Micah shuffling through some papers. "But from the motion to contest, it appears that the trust may have been set up for the unknown heirs of someone that wouldn't've been an heir to Mr. Wagner. Someone I'm guessing that was named in the trust, but was already deceased."

"How is that?" Miss Vivee asked.

"If you mean, why they did that," Micah said, "then it would probably be because either the heirs weren't born yet, like a pretermitted child or children, or that the name of the heirs were not yet known."

"Could it have been the wife who the land was left to?" Miss Vivee asked.

"Not if her name is Camren Wagner. Because she's the one contesting the trust. And . . ." Micah paused. "Yep, looks like this was filed the day after he died. Time stamped at 8:30 am. Right when court opened."

"She sure didn't waste any time, huh?" I said.

"Like she knew he was going to die," Miss Vivee muttered.

"Nope, looks like it was already ready to go, too," Micah said, evidently not hearing Miss Vivee's comment. "I mean they wrote the motion and got it filed in less than twenty-for hours. What time did he die?"

"Mid-afternoon," Mac said.

"What about all that other stuff in there?" I asked. "I sent a lot of stuff."

"Yeah, I know. So. Uhm. This just looks like stuff to open probate – application to administer the estate, appointment of appraiser, notice of probate, list of next of kin who would inherit intestate – usual, ordinary stuff."

None of it sounded ordinary to me.

"Okay, brother. I guess that's it then. Thank you."

"You're welcome," he said. "Glad to help."

I hung up and Miss Vivee gave me the evil eye. "What?" I said.

"How do you know I didn't have more questions?"

"Did you?"

"No," she said. "But he was talking so fast, it was taking a minute for my brain to catch up. I might've come up with a question."

"Then we'll call him back."

"One thing I did get," Miss Vivee said. "Is that I need to talk to that lying Camren Wagner again."

"When?" I asked.

"Now," she said. "Take me to Krieger Arboretum."

Oh brother.

Chapter Twenty-Seven

I kept my fingers crossed that Robert Bernard hadn't hopped into that pretty red roadster of his and was headed over to see Camren Wagner to check on that lie Miss Vivee had told him. He would've made it there before we could and we would have been busted. Although, in my heart, I believed that Miss Vivee could talk her way out of anything.

I brought a map of my land," Miss Vivee said and waved the blue print container at Camren Wagner. "But I've gotten a little worried."

"Worried?" Camren Wagner asked. We had arrived at the arboretum and drove straight over to where we'd seen her before, if Gavin Tanner was in the office, we didn't stop to check. We parked in the lot by the side of the greenhouses and found her sitting on her three-legged stool planting flowers.

"Well, I know that you're going to let that freckled fellow that was here the other day develop some land that you inherited from your husband. Build condos on." Miss Vivee shook her head. *"Tsk. Tsk Tsk.* I thought you were going to plant flowers. We don't want our land to be used like that."

"Why whatever do you mean?" She said, her accent heavier than ever.

"I mean the land over there at the fairgrounds. We saw Robert Bernard at the Probate Court in Augusta. He told us that you were selling him that land."

Why does she keep telling these lies that are so easily verified?

I knew, just as soon as we left, Widow Wagner was going to call Freckle Face and the two of them would compare notes and out all of Miss Vivee's lies.

"I'm not selling him-" she started in a huff.

"It is your land, isn't it?" Miss Vivee asked. "Lincoln Park?"

"Of course it is. I'm his wife. *Was* his wife," she corrected herself. "Who else would it go to?"

"Do you need money?" Miss Vivee asked. "We could help you if you need it. Although, my husband here told me that your husband was pretty well off, even without the land."

"Now you're meddling in my personal business. I have my own money." She put her hands on her hips. "I've never needed anything from Jack. Still don't."

"Oh, I didn't mean anything by that." Miss Vivee put a hand on Camren's arm to calm her. "That's why my daughter's got me going to that doctor for the elderly." She looked at Mac.

"Geriatrician," he filled in the word.

"Geriatrician," Miss Vivee repeated.

The last time we were here she told that woman she didn't have any children. Geesh.

"I have to go see one because I don't have a filter. I just say whatever pops into my brain." She tapped herself on the temple with her little bony fist.

"Well," Camren Wagner started to speak.

"Please, Dear," Miss Vivee said. "Don't be upset, and hold this against us. This is real." She held up her container. "And we just want it to be well taken care of when we're gone. You said you have your own money, right?" Camren nodded. "So, then you know what it means to try and protect what you have."

"I think she understands, Dear," Con Artist Mac said.

"But I was wondering, who is this Krieger person that the gardens are named for?" Miss Vivee said. "They won't get our land will they? You're the gardener here, that's obvious, and I want you to have it." Miss Vivee smiled at her. "Is Krieger your maiden name?"

"Oh no." Camren shook her head. "My maiden name is Smith. Actually, Krieger is my late husband's mother's name."

Hadn't Gavin told us that?

"Oh," Miss Vivee said. "Is that the Smiths of Savannah?"

"Savannah? No. We're from Pottstown."

"Well, when we leave you our land, we're going to have a section named after you. Smith Gardens we'll call it."

"Aww, thank you," Camren said. I think she evened blushed. Miss Vivee rubbed Camren's arm lightly.

"And yes. I do know what it means to try and protect what you have," Camren said.

"So maybe you can help me with the other thing I was confused about."

"There's more?" Widow Wagner lifted an eyebrow.

"Yes. I spoke to Martha Simmons the other day. You know, Aunt Martha?"

"Yes," Camren said. "Of course I know her."

"And she told me that your husband had planned on not allowing the fair to be held in Lincoln Park anymore. She was really quite upset about it. In tears and all. You know she's always been the star of the Sweet Contest."

Now where did that come from? I thought. We never did find out why Aunt Martha was crying that day we went back to the fair grounds.

"Well that's a lot of bull crap," Camren Wagner said. She folded her arms across her chest.

"I don't know . . ." Miss Vivee let her voice drift.

"You see." Mac took up her yarn. "The fair not being held there anymore just went with what Mr. Bernard told us about bulldozing the place. Another piece to the puzzle, so to speak. We wouldn't want Martha not to have a place to sell her pies."

"That's her only source of income, those pies,"

"Well I won't have any control over that," Widow Wagner said. "I'm not going to stop the fair from being there. But, I'm going to have it surveyed and hopefully named an historical district. So it'll be up to the State of Georgia whether it's ever held there again or not, not me."

"Can't you still do whatever you want with it? As the owner, I mean," I said. "The National Historic Registry doesn't place any restrictions on the use by the owner." I had learned something from my research the night before.

"Yes. I know. And I . . . Well when the time comes, I'll decided what I'll do. But to rest your mind, Mrs. Caspard-Whitson, I won't be putting any condos on it." She jutted out her chin. "I'm quite fond of that land. And I don't know about Martha's sources of income. She has her granddaughter and she's got that cookbook coming out. Or so I heard."

"A cookbook?" Miss Vivee said.

Ahhh, something Nosey Nellie doesn't know about.

"Yes. Family recipes or something. I don't know how well that'll go though, because it was Jack that made sure she won every year." Camren sucked her teeth. "So that's all she needs to worry about now – can she bake an award winning pie without Jack's help."

"Do tell," Mac said. Miss Vivee had gotten quiet.

"Look," Widow Wagner blew out a breath. "If you want to leave the land to me, do that. Draw up the papers, have you lawyer call my lawyer, or whatever it is that needs to be done. But really, I have to get back to work."

Chapter Twenty-Eight

We left the arboretum and I got Miss Vivee buckled in and held the door open for Mac. Miss Vivee was quiet. She hardly had said a word the last few minutes of the interrogation of Camren Wagner. But then, halfway back to Yasamee, she said, "I want to go and see Martha."

"Martha?"

"You know, Martha Simmons."

"Why?" I asked.

"Don't start that with me," she said. "Martha is an old friend and I'm worried about her. I never did find out why she was crying that day."

"You told Widow Wagner it was because of her worrying about where the fair would be held."

"Well, if you don't know by now that I lied, shame on you."

I chuckled. Miss Vivee tries to act as if she doesn't care about things. But I know she has a big heart, even if she doesn't show it often.

"Where does Aunt Martha live?" I asked.

"On the Augusta County line. Out past the fairgrounds."

"I've already passed that exit," I said. "Why didn't you tell me before?"

"I'm telling you now."

"Mac, you okay with taking a detour?" I asked.

"Of course he is," Miss Vivee said. "Why wouldn't he be?"

I glanced in the rearview mirror and Mac looked content looking out the window. He had so much patience with Miss Vivee. I decided I could, too.

I sighed, and got over in the far right lane so I could get off at the next exit and turn around.

ɛȝɛȝɛȝɛȝɛȝɛȝɛȝ

Martha Simmons' Peace Mobile was sitting in the dirt driveway of a huge, yellow farmhouse. And before I could get Miss Vivee and Mac out of the car, she and Marigold were on the porch waving, welcoming us with a smile.

"Vivienne!" Aunt Martha said and held out her arms to hug her. Miss Vivee braced herself for Martha's grasp and patted her on her back.

"Okay. Okay, Dear," Miss Vivee said pulling away. "I want you to meet Mac."

"Oh! This is your Mac?" she said and went to hug him.

Mac stepped back. "My pleasure, Martha," he said and tipped an imaginary hat.

"And you remember Logan," Miss Vivee said.

"Bay's girl," Aunt Martha said.

I guess my only claim to fame.

"Are you going to invite us in," Miss Vivee asked.

"Oh goodness," Aunt Martha said and clutched her chest. "Where are my manners. "Come on in." She pulled open the screen door and waved us past. We milled around in the front room, until Martha directed us to the living room.

It was big, with big furniture. All, I was sure, from the early 1900s. We stood in limbo as she gave Marigold instructions. "Go and get that pitcher of sweet tea from the icebox, and bring glasses with ice," she said. "You want some tea, don't you Vivienne?"

"That would be nice," Miss Vivee said. "I'm parched. Been talking to crazy people all afternoon. And Mac and Logan would like a glass, too."

Marigold had waited to make sure her tea getting wouldn't be in vain. After Miss Vivee confirmed, she headed to the back of the house.

"Bring the tall glasses," Aunt Martha shouted after her. She turned back and looked at us. "Have a seat. Oh my! You're just standing around. Sit! Please, sit."

"We just thought we'd pop in for a spell, Martha," Miss Vivee said.

"Well, you stay long enough to drink your tea, won't you?"

"Of course," Miss Vivee said. She wiggled down in her seat and got comfortable. "I've been thinking about you ever since I saw you at the fairgrounds that day Logan and I happened upon you."

"We're too far up in age not to keep up with friends, Vivienne. We'll have to make plans, and not just visit when we bump into each other."

"I think that's a good idea, Martha. And I want to have you, and Marigold, out to the Maypop for lunch. Real soon. Soon like tomorrow or the next day. Give you a chance to let someone else do the cooking."

"Renmar's a great cook," Aunt Martha said. "But I know she learned all she knows from you."

Miss Vivee laughed. "You could never convince her of that. She thinks she knows it all."

Miss Vivee can cook? Who knew?

Aunt Martha laughed just as Marigold walked in with a tray filled with our drinks.

"Pass them out, Marigold."

Miss Vivee took a sip of her iced tea. "Mmmm good, Martha."

"You like it?" Aunt Martha asked.

"It hits the spot," Miss Vivee said. "So, I was wondering, Dear." She sat her glass down on a coaster on the table next to her. "Why were you crying the last time I saw you?"

"Crying?" Aunt Martha tilted her head thinking. "Oh," she said. "I remember now. I had lost my diary."

"Not a diary, Nana," Marigold spoke for the first time. "It's a journal."

"Marigold with her fancy words," Aunt Martha said and waved her hand. "A journal with my recipes. Marigold found it at a yard sale. All filled with pie recipes. It's very old, mostly handwritten with some that are pasted in. You wouldn't believe the wonderful pie recipes in it. Unbelievable."

"I say," Miss Vivee said a smile came over her face. "And you had lost it?"

"I thought I had, but Marigold found it. I'm getting so old, I lose everything. My glasses, my keys. I'd forget my head if it wasn't attached," she said.

"But you've got Marigold," Miss Vivee said.

"Oh yes. She can get a little bossy sometimes, but I know it's for my own good. And she always thinking of me, like giving me that journal of recipes. I don't know what I would do without her."

"So you weren't sad that day?" Miss Vivee asked.

"Oh no!" Aunt Martha said. "Those were tears of joy."

"Seems to me, I smell something baking now," Mac said.

Oh please, God, don't let it be a cherry pie . . .

"Good nose, Mac," Aunt Martha said. "I just took an apple pie out of the oven. Dutch Apple."

And did your recipe call for apple seeds, too?

"How would you like some pie?" Aunt Martha asked.

"Yes!" Miss Vivee said and clapped her hands together. "Mac and I would love a piece."

"I'll get it, Nana," Marigold said. "And how about you, Logan? Would you like a piece?"

"None for Logan, thanks Marigold," Miss Vivee said. "She's on a diet, she's got a wedding dress to fit into."

There she goes, making me an unwanted participant in her tall tales.

This time I didn't care though, I wouldn't touch Martha Simmons pie with a ten foot pole.

"You're getting married?" Aunt Martha asked.

"That's what I'm hearing," I said.

Aunt Martha nodded with a confused look on her face.

Marigold had slipped out and was back in no time with a piping hot pie, a butcher knife and three plates. She laid them down and went and sat in one of the upholstered arm chairs.

"Marigold," Miss Vivee said taking the slice of pie Martha handed her. "You're awfully quiet."

"Oh, I'm just letting my grandmother enjoy her company," Marigold said. "She doesn't have much, she's mostly baking and entering contests. She needs more people interaction."

"Well it's good that she has you here to help," Miss Vivee said.

"And that she does!" Aunt Martha said. "She takes over everything around here. Paying the bills, getting me business for my baked goods. She's the one that talked me into moving here in the first place, picked it out on a map right after her mother, my daughter

Lynn, died. God rest her soul. Then she promised she'd come here, too, once she finished school."

"And she did?" Mac asked.

"Sure did," Aunt Martha said. "She is so good to me."

"You deserve it, Nana," Marigold said. "You were meant to be taken care of better than I ever could."

"See what I mean?" Aunt Martha said. "I couldn't ask for a better granddaughter. She even volunteered at the fair so she could be there with me early because you know they only let the contestants in before the gates open. It is so nice to have a friend. Even if she is my flesh and blood."

"I say," Miss Vivee said and smiled.

Chapter Twenty-Nine

Opening the door, and walking into Miss Vivee's room was like stepping into the past. She had big, dark wood furniture, burgundy colored walls, a high post bed with a thick, over-sized, silk brocade comforter thrown over it. My favorite piece of furniture was her vanity. It was grand with an old, faded mirror, tarnished drawer pulls, and a frayed, fringed golden stool.

She was sitting on her bed when I walked by her room and she called me in. "Come here. I want to show you something," she said.

She had come up to her room as soon as we'd gotten back from Martha Simmons' place. She had been quiet – not so much so as she'd been when we left the arboretum, but unusually quiet for her.

"What do you want to show me," I asked.

She patted the bed for me to come and sit by her. I sat next to her and she handed me a scrapbook.

"What's this?" I asked.

"Memories," she said.

The book was filled with thick parchment-colored card stock, and every page was full of pictures, programs, and mementos.

"Look," she said and pointed to a picture that looked to be from the mid-nineties. "That's me and Martha."

"Really?" I said. I bent over the book and got a closer look. They were standing next to each other on a beach.

"That's when she first came to Augusta County."

"How come she didn't know Mac?"

"She knew of him, but right after she arrived is when I became a recluse. Didn't leave the house. But that didn't stop Martha. She'd come and see me all the time."

"And look at this," Miss Vivee said. She flipped over a few pages and stabbed at a black and white. "That's me made up like a Voodoo Priestess."

"You're not one," I said. "Are you?"

"Don't act as if you don't know me," she said. "Of course I'm not. I'm an herbalist. I just add the moniker Voodoo on it. But you know one did train me."

"Yes. I remember you telling me that." I rubbed my finger over Miss Vivee's face. She was all made up with a feather headdress on. But I could see that she had been young when it was taken. Her now gray hair was dark and shoulder length.

"Is that when you found out your destiny?" I said. "Our shared destiny."

"When that first murder happened here back in '51, I thought that's when you'd come. Or at least the person that I was destined to meet. But then no one else got killed."

"You act as if that's a bad thing."

She looked at me and frowned. "Of course it's not a bad thing. I don't want anyone to die. I'm a healer. But death is going to come, and for some it'll be a violent death. So for some reason it was foretold to me that a wave of murder would blow through my way. And it would be up to me to help those souls find a peaceable cross-over. I prepared for it."

"I never heard you be so . . . I don't know – spiritual."

She chuckled. "Nothing spiritual about it. Just prepared."

"I didn't prepare," I said. "If this is a real thing, that it's my – our – destiny, then I didn't sign on for it. I didn't prepare for it, and I don't want to do it."

"Sure you did." She nodded at me. "Everything you did up to the point you found me was preparation."

"I always thought that I must've been meant to be here to meet Bay."

"Ah, because he's your soulmate," she said as more of a statement than a question.

I giggled. "Is he my soul mate?" I scrunched my nose.

She patted my hand. "It was *all* meant to be."

"If you say so, Miss Vivee."

Abby L. Vandiver

"And you'll take the things you've learned from the time you spend here with me, and they will help you to do great things in your life."

"I don't care so much about that." I looked at her. "At least, not as much as I used to." I shook my head. I had so many emotions going on inside of me, I didn't even know how to explain it out loud. I couldn't even sort it out in my own mind. I went back to her idea of our so-called shared destiny. "So how many murders are there supposed to be?"

"I don't know."

"Lord give me strength," I mumbled under my breath. "Well, do you at least know how long this 'wave of death' as you call it, will last?"

"Nope."

"Crap."

"Only thing I know for sure was that the first murder here, not the first murder I'd seen mind you, way back when wasn't the start of it."

"How do you know that for sure?"

"Because you didn't show up for another half century," she said.

I laughed. "Maybe it was meant as a forecaster. Of things to come," I said. "Maybe you were supposed to learn something from it. Something that would help in the coming murders. Did you work on the case?"

"No," she said hesitantly. "But I did write a book about it."

"You wrote a book?" It was impossible, even with the time I spent with her, to know when Miss Vivee was telling the truth. "You never told me that," I said. "You're kidding, right?"

"You never asked."

"You get it published?"

"No." She got up and went to her closet. She pulled up a low stool with short stubby legs, and started to climb onto it.

"What are you doing?" I laid the scrap book on her bed and rushed over to her. I grabbed her hand and helped her bring her one foot down.

"It's up on the shelf." She pointed. "My book. I want to show it to you."

"I'll get it," I said. "That's not safe for you to do."

"*Pshaw*," she blew out in a breath. "I climb up there all the time." She waved at the stool. "It's not even that high."

"Well, you shouldn't," I said. "You could fall and break a hip," I looked at her. "Or something."

"If I didn't do it, who'd you think would?" She cocked her head and looked at me. "I can get along just fine without any help."

"I know, Miss Vivee," I said, not wanting her to think that I thought she couldn't. I had come to learn that even with her five-foot-nothing frame, tall orders weren't too much for Miss Vivee to triumph over. "But, I'm here now," I said. "So let me do it."

I stepped up on the three-legged stool, reached up and grabbed ahold of a box on the bottom row.

"That's not it," she said watching me with an eagle eye. "It's the one right there in the middle. Right there." I turned and looked at her so she could guide me. "The black, square one with the white ribbon." She pointed. I stretched, standing up on my toes to reach for it. "That one!" she said. "Get it. Give it to me." Smiling, she reached her arms out and wiggled her fingers.

"Hold on, Miss Vivee. I don't want to knock the rest of these boxes down."

"If you do, you'll be picking them up." Her smile changed into a frown.

"Yeah. I figured that." I pulled out the one she wanted, and handed it to her. "Here," I said. Then turned back to make sure the other boxes were still securely placed. She took the box and sat back on her bed.

I stepped off the stool, and brushed my hands together. I made a mental note to come and clean that closet. I walked over and stood in front of her. "I don't see how you would have gotten that box down by yourself," I said. "I could hardly reach it."

"I can stretch nearly the length of my height," she said and nodded. "I do yoga."

"You do not," I said and rolled my eyes. "And no one can stretch that far."

"I can," she said, brushing the dust off the box.

I did wonder how she'd gotten all those boxes up there, though.

"Come sit down," she instructed. "So I can show you."

She had wanted to visit old friends, now she was going poring over memories.

Tonight seemed to be one of nostalgia for her.

She pulled the ribbon string and it unraveled easily. It had a stack of loose leaf onion-paper, all filled with words from an old typewriter. I ran my hand over the top page, I could feel the indentation of each letter from the key strokes.

"Wow," I said. "This took a lot to do."

"Yes it did." I saw a twinkle in her eye as she spoke. "It was a big uproar because there hadn't been any murders around here since the Civil War."

"People were murdered here during the war?"

"It was a war, Logan. Soldiers died."

"I don't think that casualties of war are called murders."

"Sometimes that scientific background of yours gets in the way of your thinking," Miss Vivee said. "Stop being so literal. Anyway," she took in a breath. "Her name was Lily. Lily LeGrande. Beautiful young thing. Black hair. Eyes so blue, when the light hit them, they looked violet. She looked like she could be Elizabeth Taylor's twin." She looked at me. "You know who Elizabeth Taylor is?"

"Was," I said. "She's dead, but I knew who she was."

"No! Elizabeth Taylor is dead?" her eyes wide, lips pouty. "Couldn't be. When did that happen?"

"A while ago," I assured her.

"Well, anyway, Lily looked like her. Beautiful as I said. She had a young daughter, an infant. Her name was Bella Donna LeGrande. She was just as beautiful as her mother. The night Lily was murdered they found the baby home by herself. Everyone wondered what could have been so important that she left her child and went out in the middle of the night. I guess she never figured she wouldn't be coming back."

"What happened to her?"

"I told you, somebody killed her." She patted my hand. "Try to keep up so I don't have to keep repeating myself."

"No. I mean how did she die?"

"She was strangled."

"Oh," I said.

"She was found in the field right there at the fairgrounds of Lincoln Park.

"Why would they want to have the fair there then? That's a terrible place to have it after a murder was committed there."

"No one is sure where the murder was committed. But her body was found there."

"Who found her?" I asked.

She raised her eyebrows. "You'll never believe this," she said. "It was Lincoln Wagner."

"Am I supposed to know who he is?" I said and then thought about it. "Wait. Lincoln Park. Jack Wagner. Are they related?"

"Lincoln Wagner and his son, Jackson found the body," Miss Vivee said. I guessed that was the answer to my question, but even though she didn't say it straight out, I got what I needed to know. "It was all over the newspapers." She pointed at the scrapbook. "Hand me that."

I handed to her and she seemed to flip right to the page. "Here she said."

"Wow," I said after reading the article. "That's awful." I looked at her then back down at the newspaper clipping. "So they dedicated Lincoln Park as a memorial?"

"That's why I knew about the flowers. That field of flowers that you insisted I look at in Lincoln Park," she said and gave me a glare.

"I just wanted you to be sure that those flowers from the note weren't there."

"I told you that there was only one of those flowers on that note there. You didn't believe me?" I opened my mouth to speak but before I could, she said "Or did you think me too old and senile to be sure."

"Never, Miss Vivee," I said and smiled. "I'd never think that about you."

I scolded myself, because maybe that really was what I had thought, and there was no reason for me to ever think that about Vivienne Pennywell.

"So like I said those lilies were planted in her memory and the fair started being there after that." She said and closed her scrapbook. "That's why it's called the Freemont County Fair. It used to be in Freemont County. Moved it here in her honor."

"Why is that?"

259

"She was the queen of the fair. Won every year with her pies. She had more ribbons than Woolworth's Five and Dime." Miss Vivee clasped her hands together, and licked her lips as if she was reliving the memory. "Dutch Apple, Cherry, Rhubarb. They were the best."

"All deadly," I said under my breath. I had learned a lot in the past few days about everyday foods that kill.

"They were delicious. So good, in fact, it was rumored that she'd gotten an offer to sell her pies through Flower Foods."

"Flower Foods?"

"Yep."

"Everything about this is floral."

"The Flower brothers opened it up around 1919 over in Thomasville."

"Thomasville, Georgia?"

"You know any other Thomasville?"

"No." I didn't even know that Thomasville.

"Yep, that was around the time they started freezing foods. Heard hers was going to be frozen and sold by their company. Instead, she died, and a Mrs. Smith up in Pennsylvania started selling them."

"Mrs. Smith's Pies? Now I've heard of that." I tilted my head. "I'm sure I've probably even eaten a few. They're good."

"Lily's pies were to die for," Miss Vivee said. "No pun intended."

"No pun taken," I said.

"You should read it," she said and put the box with her manuscript on my lap.

"You want me to read it?" I asked.

"Yes," she said. "I think you should." She looked me in the eyes. "But you have to promise me you'll read it tonight."

"Tonight?" I lifted the box, checking the weight. "This seems like an awful lot to read in one night."

"I have faith in you. I think you can do anything that you put your mind to." She smiled and patted my cheek. "So you promise?" she said.

"Promise," I said.

Chapter Thirty

"Jack Wagner's murder wasn't about his land," I said standing in the doorway to Miss Vivee's bedroom early the next morning. I hadn't slept all night. I wanted to keep my promise

"No it wasn't," Miss Vivee said. She was sitting at her vanity. Her long white hair hanging loose. "And that note wasn't a red herring."

"It really was a clue to the murderer." I came into her room and sat the black box on her bed. I had neatly tied the white ribbon back, and tried to make the contents look undisturbed. Cat was laying on the bed, she looked like she wasn't ready to get up yet.

"Just like you said, Logan," Miss Vivee gave a nod. "Here," she said and picked up her hairbrush. "Come and brush my hair."

I walked over and took the brush from her and ran it through her silky hair.

So, you've figured it out then?" she asked looking at me in the mirror.

"I think so," I said.

"Good. Okay," Miss Vivee said and took the brush. "Braid it, and help me get ready. We need to round up the culprit and get her here."

"You want them both?" I asked.

"Yep." She nodded. "First though, I need you to look up somethings for me on that phone of yours. We've got to have all our ducks in a row. After that I want you to get them here. Then call Bay and Sheriff Haynes. Tell them we've got the killer here waiting for them."

ƐƷƐƷƐƷƐƷƐƷƐƷƐƷ

"It was Lincoln Wagner who killed Lily LeGrande sixty-five years ago." Miss Vivee announced. "And his son Jackson saw it happen."

"Grandmother," Bay said slowly. "What are you doing?"

"Solving your case," Miss Vivee said then looked over at Sheriff Haynes. "And Yasamee's only cold case."

I had called Martha Simmons and her granddaughter, Marigold and invited them to that lunch Miss Vivee had promised them. They readily agreed, but was taken aback when they walked in the door and saw the Sheriff.

Bay was the last to come in. He had looked around the foyer, his mouth open, hands on hips. Miss Vivee and I were sitting on our beige tufted bench near at the front door. It was where we always sat when we solved our murders. Cat at her feet. Aunt Martha stood in the middle of the floor clutching her chest, surprise on her face. Marigold seemed to have a smirk.

"Don't go making accusations," Bay said.

"No accusations, Grandson. Just the truth. Sixty-five years later."

"The truth?" Aunt Martha said. "What is the truth, Vivienne?"

"The truth is that Marigold killed Jack Wagner."

Everyone let out a collective gasp. Including me.

Miss Vivee must've noticed the surprised look on my face. "You thought it was Martha, didn't you?" she said to me.

"Yeah. I kind of did," I said.

"I told you," she said. "Martha couldn't hurt a fly. Could you, Martha?"

"Of course not," Aunt Martha said. "And neither could Marigold." She went over and looped her arm around Marigold's shoulder.

"It's okay, Nana," Marigold said and wiggled out of grandmother's grasp. "They don't have any proof."

"Proof?" Aunt Martha said. "Why would you say that, Marigold?" Tears were forming in her eyes. "Tell them that you didn't do it."

"Grandmother," Bay said. "What proof do *you* have?"

"DNA," Miss Vivee said.

"You're conducting DNA analysis now?" Bay asked. "In what? Your own forensic lab?"

"Don't get smart with me. I'm thankful that my grandchild is not a murderer," she looked over at

Marigold and back at Bay. "But I won't tolerate no sass," Miss Vivee said.

"Tell me what you got, Miss Vivee," Sheriff Haynes said. "Because I know you couldn't conduct a DNA test."

"No. I can't. But Logan looked up for me how to unseal adoption records," Miss Vivee said and patted my hand. "It seems that for sealed adoptions, like the one that happened for Lily LeGrande's daughter, papers must be filed with the court to get any information that would identify the biological parents. But for unidentifying information like where they were born, you don't need a court order. Isn't that right, Marigold?"

"I wouldn't know," she said, that stupid smirk still on her face.

"So Miss Marigold Kent got that unidentifying information. Found out her grandmother was born in Augusta County and starting searching all the public records she could find. Lily's death, and the fact she had an infant daughter, was in all the newspapers. Probably wasn't too hard to deduce that Martha might just be Bella Donna." Miss Vivee looked at Marigold. "Especially after Martha couldn't give you the information you needed for your genealogy study."

"All the information she gave me checked out. It was her adoptive family's information."

"My adoptive family?" Aunt Martha said. "I wasn't adopted."

"Yes you were," Marigold nodded her head. "I found the adoption papers in your parents – adopted parents' boxes you had stored."

"I'd told you I would go through those boxes," Aunt Martha said.

"I had just wanted to help," Marigold said.

"So why didn't you tell me? After you found out, why didn't you show me what you'd found" Aunt Martha looked at Marigold, but she said nothing. "Bella Donna?" Aunt Martha repeated the words and shook her head. "Isn't that something that people use to poison with?"

"Yes," Miss Vivee said. "And it's your birth name."

"Nightshade," I said. "Is another name for it."

Miss Vivee looked at Sheriff Haynes. He nodded his head. "And that flower was in that poem," he said.

"So was the lily of the valley," Miss Vivee said. "And all the time I thought whoever wrote that note couldn't spell. Putting an 'e' on grand." Miss Vivee looked at Marigold. "L-E-G-R-A-N-D-E. You spelled 'grand' like her – like your great-grandmother's last name. That's why you put an 'e' on it. Isn't it."

"That would be your only clue," Marigold said quoting the poem.

"I need to sit down," Aunt Martha said. "I think that I'm going to faint." Aunt Martha's knees drooped and she grabbed her head.

Sheriff Haynes and Bay moved toward her, and Marigold moved toward the door.

"Hold on there, young lady," Sheriff Haynes said and slid back in front of the door blocking Marigold. "You got Martha, Bay?"

"Yeah, I got her," Bay said. He held onto her and walked with her over to the registration counter. "Lean on this, Mrs. Simmons. I'll get something for you to sit in." He went into the dining room off the foyer and brought her a chair and got her settled in it. "Now, Grandmother, you were saying about DNA."

"If you check Martha's DNA against that of Lily's, you'll see that they're related."

"We don't have any DNA from Lily LeGrande, Grandmother," Bay said. "Do we?" he looked at Sheriff Haynes.

"Not sure. But I doubt it. That was a long time ago. Way before we knew anything about DNA."

"You got anything else, Grandmother?" Bay said.

"Don't be so quick now, Bay." Miss Vivee nodded her head toward Martha. "She's got a journal. It's old and it's filled with recipes. Some handwritten, some pasted in. Someone had to lick them, because back then we didn't have self-adhesive cards. I'm suspecting that is was Lily who did it, that's why Marigold checked Martha's DNA."

Everyone looked over at Marigold.

She chuckled. "Wasn't hard to get her to sign the papers to get the record unsealed, but I had to come up with a big story for her to let me swab the inside of her cheek."

"Why did she kill him, Grandmother?" Bay asked.

"Oh, good heavens!" Aunt Martha said and slumped in her chair.

"Mrs. Simmons are you going to be alright?" Bay asked.

"No! I don't know that I'll ever be alright again." Aunt Martha pulled a wad of tissues from her purse and swiped them across her head. "Hearing all of this is killing me. It just couldn't be true. Could it?" She looked at Marigold then swung around in her chair and looked at Miss Vivee. "Could it?"

"Well, I'm going to have to hear my grandmother out," Bay said. "So if you don't think you can listen – can take it – then I can have Logan wait with you in the other room."

And miss Miss Vivee in action? Sorry, Bay but you're going to have to come up with another plan.

"No. No," Aunt Martha said. "I don't want to go." She looked over at Marigold. "She's my granddaughter. She may need my help."

"Don't worry, Nana. They don't have anything on me."

"Grandmother," Bay said. "How did you come to this conclusion?"

"Lily LeGrande baked pies like nobody's business. She kept all her recipes in a journal. She showed it to me once. I'm sure that the one that Martha has is one and the same."

"Did you see Mrs. Simmons' journal?" Sheriff Haynes asked.

"Nope," Miss Vivee said. But I've tasted her Dutch Apple pie, and it's Lily's."

"That does not a murderer make, Grandmother." Bay said. "And a DNA match between Mrs. Simmons and Lily LeGrande doesn't prove that Marigold killed anyone."

"Marigold gave Martha that journal. I remember they looked all over for it after the murder, and no one could find it. I suspect it been taken so Lincoln Wagner could share its contents with the Smiths of Pottstown."

"Pottstown?" I said. "Where Camren Wagner is from? I thought she meant Pottstown, Georgia."

"Have you ever heard of a Pottstown, Georgia?" Miss Vivee asked me.

I hadn't heard of Pottstown, Pennsylvania either.

"So, that's Camren Wagner's family?" I asked. I wanted to keep the story moving.

"Yes. Remember you said that you'd eaten a few Mrs. Smith's pies, Logan. Ever had their Dutch Apple?"

"Wait. Are you saying . . ." I looked at Miss Vivee. This part wasn't in her book. "Are you saying that Jack Wagner married a woman from the Smith family? The ones that make the frozen pies?"

"Yes."

"Sooo . . ." I was trying to put it all together. "Lincoln Wagner took Lily's pie recipes-"

"And her idea for frozen pies," Marigold said.

We all looked at her.

269

"He took them . . ." I was still gathering my thoughts.

"Killed her for them," Miss Vivee said. "While his son watched."

"I didn't work that case," Sheriff Haynes said. "Wasn't even born yet. But I've read the file. I know that it was Lincoln Wagner that found her. He, I think, said he and his boy were out walking when they discovered the body."

"He's the one that put the body there," Miss Vivee said.

"Do you have any proof of that?" Bay asked.

"Proof of that could have only came from Jack Wagner. But it seems like little Miss Marigold made it so we wouldn't be able to hear any of that from him," Miss Vivee said. "He probably had confessed it to her when she went to ask him about finding her great-grandmother's body. And when he gave her the recipe book."

"Had you ever spoken to Jack Wagner?" Bay directed his question to Marigold.

"We've had words."

"And did he tell you he was really sorry. So sorry that he'd never came forward. So sorry that he planted lilies all over that field at Lincoln Park?" Miss Vivee asked.

"Yep. So sorry he said," Marigold answered the question, "that he set up a trust, leaving the land to Lily LeGrande's heirs. And then he found out her heir was my grandmother. He said he was so remorseful that he hadn't spoken up."

"He was only five at the time it happened," Miss Vivee said.

"He grew up," Marigold said. Her eyebrows knitted together, her breathing so heavy she sounded as if she was snorting. "Planting lilies, and bequeathing land. *Hmph!*"

"You didn't care anything about that land, did you?" Miss Vivee asked.

"No," Marigold said. "Or those stupid lilies. Jackson Wagner's father stole my grandmother's legacy."

"I wouldn't have cared about that!" Aunt Martha screeched. "I didn't even know anything about my legacy."

"So what about everyone getting sick at the fair, Miss Vivee," Sheriff Haynes asked. "Did she do that too?"

"Yes she did," Miss Vivee nodded and looked at Marigold. "That's why Martha couldn't find that recipe journal of hers."

"I misplaced it," Aunt Martha said. "I told you that, Vivienne."

"Marigold took it," Miss Vivee said. "She wanted to bake a special pie for Jack Wagner. One of Lily's very own creations." She looked at Marigold and smiled. "But with a special ingredient – the addition of amygdalin. Sprinkled right on top." Miss Vivee shook her head. "You learned that with that nutrition degree, didn't you. The one you got from the University of California." She looked over at the sheriff. "I don't know why she wanted everyone else to get sick."

Aunt Martha looked at Marigold, it seemed, for the first time, with disgust. "You made all those people sick?"

"I didn't want that fair to be there anymore. Jack Wagner making money off of the memory of my great-grandmother." She hissed. "All he had to do was the right thing."

"Why did you write that note, Marigold?" Bay asked. "Did you want to get caught?"

"I did it for fun," she said. "It was the perfect murder and I was proud of it. I didn't think anyone could have figured out I did it," she said.

"That's because you didn't know about my grandmother," Bay said.

Epilogue

Without someone knowing Lily LeGrande personally, Marigold would have figured correctly, no one could have guessed she'd did it.

That's why it's never good to mess with old people. They've been around a long time, and they know a lot of stuff.

And no one but a Voodoo herbalist, or the owner of an arboretum would have all nine of those poisonous flowers in their garden. But we figured out it was just a coincidence that they had those flowers. Marigold just needed to include Nightshade and Lily in her poem. And spell amygdalin.

Miss Vivee said Marigold popped into her head when she saw that blonde in Robert Bernard's car. She said she didn't know why, but then all the pieces started to fall into place. That manuscript of hers didn't hurt either. As soon as I read it, even I knew "whodunit." Well, almost. I had thought it was Aunt Martha.

I finally got the chance to call my parents after my weird engagement dinner. Bay had purchased the tickets for the following weekend. Once I got over the shock of no ring, and the stomach ache from that seven layer, decadent chocolate cake, I asked him why he'd planned the trip so soon, especially since he was in the middle of a murder investigation. He told me that he knew it wouldn't take long for me and his grandmother to figure it out.

I punched him.

He gives the two of us so much grief about "nosing around" in his investigations. Always telling us to stay out of the murder solving business. I guess I was naive to think that he believed we listened.

I decided not to pack any clothes to go home. I had plenty of stuff to wear there, in fact, I needed to bring more of my things back with me on my return. But the closer it got to the time to go home, the more anxious I got.

I was anxious about facing my mother. I was anxious about getting that ring, and I was anxious about being someone's wife.

I hadn't been on any excavations lately, and other than helping Miss Vivee solve murders, I wasn't doing much else with my life. Now I was going to get engaged. Being a housewife in itself was a full time job. Or so I've been told.

And to top that all off, Miss Vivee gave Bay and I an early wedding gift. It turned out her tall tale of inheriting Capt. Albert Caspard's grant of land in the

Black Belt was all true (except for the *thousands* of acres part, it was only a few hundred). Complete, she tells me, with a plantation, and she gave it to us.

Black plantation owners. Go figure.

And she really did want to have it nominated for an historic place, and thought that if those "lying no-good Goodalls" could do the archaeological research for the National Registry, then so could I.

Sigh.

My mother juggled being married, raising a family and a career all at the same time, so I figured if she could do it . . .

There I go again, trying to compete with my mother.

I remembered how she would drag us along on her digs, three kids and my dad, and she didn't miss a beat. And my father used to joke that he'd follow her anywhere, all he needed was a laptop and a modem. But he wrote a syndicated sports column. He didn't have to sit in an office, or spend days at a crime scene like Bay. Bay's job was not mobile.

And what about my "destiny?"

According to Miss Vivee, I was born to be Nancy Drew.

And we both had concluded that Lily LeGrande's death sixty-five years earlier was when our shared destiny began. Even though I wasn't even born yet. It was to be solved by us.

Okay, so I was starting to buy into that idea a little.

275

Suddenly, I wanted to go home. Couldn't wait. I needed my mother's help. Again.

The End.

Thank you for taking time to read *Food Fair Frenzy*. Look for the rest of the books in the Logan Dickerson Cozy Mystery Series coming soon. If you enjoyed it, please consider telling your friends about it. And don't forget to take the time to click on the link and post a short review.

http://amzn.to/2blGgne

A Note from the Author

It's been a year since I've written about Logan and Miss Vivee, but they're back with more to follow. So, be sure to follow them on their quirky, fun filled adventures. They'll be filled with mystery, murder and even a little romance.

Logan Dickerson is the daughter of the main character in my *Mars Origin "I" Series*. (So if you like mysteries with just a touch of sci-fi, you might want to check them out!). Logan is from Ohio (like me), but her stories are based in Georgia. I love the coastline there and thought it would be a perfect setting for a cozy mystery.

In this installment, the gang is back in Yasamee. And as usual there is a little real history, and real places. For instance, Miss Vivee talks about the Black Belt. The Black Belt is a region in the Southern United States. It was eventually developed for cotton plantations based on slave labor and the term became associated with the agricultural region. And there is a mall with Walmart and Dillards on Wrightsboro Road in Augusta, as well as the John H. Ruffin, Jr. Courthouse. And Frog Hollow Tavern and their signature drink, the Tea Hive is real, too. Next time you're in Augusta, check it out.

Thanks to all my beta reader, Kathryn Dionne. As always, the book is better because of you.

I appreciate all my reviews and look forward to reading what you thought about my book. Grammatical errors are of course unintended, so if you find any, just email me and let me know what you've found.

I love connecting with my readers and look forward to chatting with you.

Read My Other Books

Coastal Cottage Calamity – A Logan Dickerson
Cozy Mystery
http://amzn.to/1SvL1Z4

Maya Mound Mayhem – A Logan Dickerson Cozy
Mystery
http://amzn.to/1fah16e

In the Beginning: Mars Origin "I" Series Book I
http://amzn.to/1cwDnd2

Irrefutable Proof: Mars Origin "I" Series Book II
http://amzn.to/1bwWjFt

Incarnate: Mars Origin "I" Series Book III
http://amzn.to/1y2Soy0

At the End of the Line
http://amzn.to/1fg7DYy

Mysticism and Myths
http://amzn.to/1tcCUCn

Get a FREE eBook of my first novel, In the Beginning, when you sign up for my newsletter. I'll never spam you, I promise, you'll just get updates on my books. Visit my website at www.abbyvandiver.com to get your book

What if the history you learned in school wasn't the truth?

2,000 year old manuscripts, a reluctant archaeologists, a world changing discovery . . .
In the Beginning, an alternative history story.

Made in the USA
Monee, IL
02 August 2021

74787862R00171